# 100 MUST-READ
# CRIME
# FICTION NOVELS

Richard Shephard and Nick Rennison

Windsor and Maidenhead

A &

First published 2006

5 7 9 10 8 6 4

A & C Black Publishers Limited
38 Soho Square
London W1D 3HB
www.acblack.com

© 2006 Richard Shephard and Nick Rennison

ISBN 978−0−7136−7584−9

A CIP catalogue record for this book is available from
the British Library.

This book is produced using paper that is made from wood grown in
managed, sustainable forests. It is natural, renewable and recyclable.
The logging and manufacturing processes conform to the environmental
regulations of the country of origin.

Typeset in 8.5pt on 12pt Meta-Light

Printed in the UK by CPI Bookmarque, Croydon, CR0 4TD

# CONTENTS

ABOUT THIS BOOK . . . . . . . . . . . . . . . . . . . . . . . . . . v

INTRODUCTION . . . . . . . . . . . . . . . . . . . . . . . . . . . ix

A–Z OF ENTRIES . . . . . . . . . . . . . . . . . . . . . . . . . . . 1

CRIME FICTION AWARDS . . . . . . . . . . . . . . . . . . . 159

INDEX . . . . . . . . . . . . . . . . . . . . . . . . . . . . . . . . . . 164

# ABOUTTHISBOOK

This book is not intended to provide a list of the 100 'best' crime novels. Any such definitive list is an impossibility, given the huge variety of fiction that is classified as 'crime fiction' and the difficulty of directly comparing books which were written with very different intentions and in very different cultural circumstances. How is it possible to take, say, a Lord Peter Wimsey novel by Dorothy L. Sayers and one of James Ellroy's LA Quartet and say which of them is 'the best'? Both may fall within the broad church of crime fiction but comparing them directly is as useful as comparing apples and pears. Some like apples; some like pears. Some like both. We have been guided instead by the title of our book and have chosen 100 books to read in order to gain an overview of the rich and diverse writing to be found in crime fiction. We aimed to produce a book that would prove useful as a starting point for exploring the genre, and the introduction attempts the difficult, if not impossible, task of galloping through the history of crime fiction in a few thousand words.

The individual entries are arranged A to Z by author. They describe the plot of each title while aiming to avoid too many 'spoilers', offer some value judgements and usually include some information about the author's career and their place in the history of crime fiction. We have noted significant film versions of the books (with dates of release), where applicable.

Each entry is followed by a 'Read On' list which includes books by the same author, books by stylistically similar writers or books on a theme relevant to the entry. We have also included 20 'Read on a theme' lists, which are scattered throughout the text after appropriate titles; these are designed to help you to explore a particular subgenre of, or theme in, crime fiction in greater depth. The symbol » before an author name (e.g. » James Lee Burke) indicates that one or more of their books is covered in the A to Z author entries.

Most authors receive one entry only. Originally we intended to have 100 authors and 100 books but we decided eventually that three writers (Raymond Chandler, Agatha Christie and Sir Arthur Conan Doyle) were so central to the genre that they deserved two entries. We have also ignored the constraints of our title by including three short-story collections which we believe are essential to a full understanding of the history of crime fiction. Edgar Allan Poe's stories played a major role in the genesis of the genre and he could not be excluded simply because he did not write a novel-length crime story. Conan Doyle wrote four novels and 56 short stories in which Sherlock Holmes appears and it seemed right to select as our two choices one of the longer stories and one of the collections of short stories. G.K. Chesterton's Father Brown is one of the most loved and admired detectives in English crime fiction and it would have been misguided to leave him out of the guide solely on the grounds that he appears only in short stories.

For writers who have written many books, choosing just one to represent their work has proved difficult. Some writers have produced long series featuring the same character. In most cases, the earlier books in the series are the freshest and most inspired and we have chosen one of these but that is not always so. To represent Elizabeth Peters, for example, we have selected the first in her Amelia Peabody series, but to represent Ian Rankin, we have gone for *Black and Blue*, a later book in his Rebus series. Some writers have, in the course of long careers, produced books in a number of series and in a number of styles. Here the difficulty has been in choosing which series to highlight. In all cases we have chosen the series for which, in our opinion, the writer is most likely to find his place in the history of crime fiction. Robert B. Parker, for example, has written a very fine series of books featuring an ex-alcoholic cop named Jesse Stone but it is his novels starring the hip, wisecracking private eye Spenser that first made his name and which remain his most famous. However tempting it was to choose a Jesse Stone novel rather than a Spenser novel to represent Parker, it would have seemed deliberately perverse and unnecessarily controversial to do so.

All the first choice books in this guide have a date attached to them. In the case of English and American writers, this date refers to the first publication in the UK or the USA. For translated writers, dates of publication refer to the book's first appearance in English.

# INTRODUCTION

What is crime fiction? The simplest definition would be one that states that it is fiction in which a crime plays the central role in the plot. However, closer examination of this definition shows it to be inadequate. In *Oliver Twist*, many of the novel's most compelling scenes take place in London's criminal underworld and Bill Sikes's murder of Nancy is of major importance to the plot. The narrative of Dostoevsky's *Crime and Punishment* unfolds from Raskolnikov's murder of an old pawnbroker and her sister. In a more contemporary novel, Martin Amis's *London Fields*, the anticipated murder of one of the characters is the driving force behind the plot. The first two chapters are even entitled 'The Murderer' and 'The Murderee'. Yet no one would think of describing any of these three novels as 'crime fiction'. A better definition can be achieved if we extend the previous one a little and say that crime fiction is fiction in which the unravelling and detection of the truth about a crime, usually but not exclusively murder, plays the central role in the plot.

When and where did crime fiction begin? Some students of the genre, eager to provide it with a respectably lengthy pedigree, have traced its sources back to stories in biblical and Ancient Greek literature but this is special pleading. More convincingly, the critic and crime writer Julian Symons cited William Godwin's 1794 novel *Caleb Williams* as the first true crime novel. Certainly *Caleb Williams* hinges on the investigation of a murder but Godwin is more interested in using his narrative to expose the injustices of contemporary society than he is in unfolding a suspenseful crime novel. It is difficult to read the book today and accept unreservedly that here is a work of crime fiction. A better case can be made that the genre really began in the middle decades of the nineteenth century and that it began in America, England and France.

## AN ENGLISH, A FRENCHMAN AND AN AMERICAN...

In America in the 1840s, » Edgar Allan Poe became the founding father of detective fiction with the three short stories in which the brilliantly ratiocinative Auguste Dupin solves apparently insoluble mysteries. 'The Murders in the Rue Morgue', first published in a magazine in 1841, is the prototype 'locked room mystery' in which Dupin is faced by a series of murders where the killings take place in apparently inaccessible rooms and has to work out how they were committed. It was followed by 'The Mystery of Marie Roget', in which Poe takes a notorious real-life murder in New York and re-imagines it in Dupin's Paris, and 'The Purloined Letter', the story of a compromising letter being used for blackmail, which Dupin finds after all police attempts to locate it have failed.

In England in the 1860s, a new genre of fiction emerged which became known as 'sensation fiction'. With its antecedents in the Gothic and 'Newgate' novels of earlier decades, 'sensation fiction' peered beneath the surface gentility of Victorian domesticity and revealed a world of bigamy, madness, murder and violence supposedly lurking there. It was all too much for some critics. One described the genre as 'unspeakably disgusting' and castigated its 'ravenous appetite for carrion'. The best-known purveyor of 'sensation fiction' was » Wilkie Collins. Collins's most famous books are *The Woman in White* (1860) and *The Moonstone* (1868), novels which hinge on the working out of a crime mystery. In *The Moonstone* Wilkie Collins introduces the idiosyncratic and intelligent Sergeant Cuff who, although he mistakenly suspects an innocent person and is eventually dismissed from the case, is the first of innumerable police protagonists in crime fiction over the next 140 years.

Collins may have been influenced by the short-lived French novelist Emile Gaboriau (1833–73) who wrote a number of books which use themes and motifs still recognisable in crime fiction today. A great admirer of Poe, Gaboriau is best remembered for the creation of Monsieur Lecoq, an agent of the French Sûreté and a rational, scientifi-cally minded detective able to astonish his colleagues by his careful analysis of clues at the scene of the crime and his leaps of deduction. Lecoq first appeared as a supporting character in an 1866 novel entitled *The Lerouge Affair* but he took centre stage in *The Mystery of Orcival* (1867) and several subsequent novels.

Together, the American Poe, the Englishman Collins and the French-man Gaboriau created templates in crime fiction which have lasted to the present day.

## THE INCOMPARABLE HOLMES

The next leap forward came, some twenty years after the publication of *The Moonstone* and more than a decade after the death of Gaboriau, with **»** Arthur Conan Doyle's creation of Sherlock Holmes. Holmes is not an entire original (Doyle borrowed elements from both Poe's Dupin and Gaboriau's Lecoq) but the supremely rational private investigator, able to make the most startlingly accurate deductions on the basis of the flimsiest of evidence, rapidly became the most famous of all fictional detectives, a position he has held ever since and is unlikely to relinquish as long as crime fiction is read.

Holmes and his stolid comrade Dr Watson have transcended the boundaries of the fiction in which they appeared in a way that few characters in English literature, other than some of Shakespeare's and some of Dickens's, have done. They have entered an almost mythical realm. The two men first appeared in *A Study in Scarlet*, published in *Beeton's Christmas Annual* of 1887. Doyle received the princely sum of £25 for the rights to the novella. *The Sign of Four* followed in 1890 but it was only when *The Strand* magazine began publishing Holmes short stories in 1891 that the character's enormous public popularity really began. The magazine's circulation rose dramatically as the stories were published. Eventually Doyle, wearying of his character and keen that his historical fiction should not be overshadowed by the detective, attempted to kill Holmes off, sending him hurtling over the Reichenbach Falls in the arms of his mortal enemy Professor Moriarty. But the public was having none of it. They wanted more of the great detective and Doyle had finally to acquiesce to public demand and resurrect Holmes. He continued to publish Holmes stories in *The Strand* until 1927. By this time, the Golden Age of English crime fiction was set to dawn.

# CRIME'S GOLDEN YEARS

The years between the first and last appearances of Sherlock Holmes in *The Strand* were fruitful ones for crime fiction. Holmes had plenty of imitators, from Arthur Morrison's Martin Hewitt (whose adventures also appeared in *The Strand* in the 1890s) to Jacques Futrelle's character, Professor Van Dusen, the 'Thinking Machine' who featured in a series of short stories and two novels published in the first decade of the 20th century. Many other writers enjoyed success with crime fiction. Some, like » G.K. Chesterton, who created the meek but masterly priest Father Brown in 1911, wrote their detective stories in the time they could spare from other writing. Others, like Chesterton's close friend » E.C. Bentley, produced a single, striking example of the genre (Bentley published *Trent's Last Case* in 1913). Yet others built long careers on crime fiction. R. Austin Freeman wrote *The Red Thumb Mark*, his first book about the forensic investigator and lawyer Dr Thorndyke, in 1907 and went on to publish more than 30 other novels involving the same character. Edgar Wallace's prodigious output of crime fiction (he often published half a dozen books a year) began with *The Four Just Men* in 1905 and continued until his death in Hollywood in 1932 (where he was working on the script of *King Kong*).

It was women writers, however, who led the way in creating English crime fiction's Golden Age. » Agatha Christie published her first novel, *The Mysterious Affair at Styles*, in 1920 and it introduced the character of Hercule Poirot, who was soon to become the second most famous fictional detective in the world. Other women writers followed in Christie's footsteps. » Dorothy L. Sayers's first Lord Peter Wimsey book appeared in 1923, » Margery Allingham created the character of Albert Campion in her 1929 novel *The Crime at Black Dudley* and » Ngaio

Marsh produced her first novel in 1934. By this time the rules and conventions of the classic whodunit were firmly in place. Indeed, a Detection Club for crime novelists was founded in 1928. Early members included Sayers, Christie, Chesterton and Ronald Knox and they agreed, half in jest and half in earnest, to adhere to a set of rules in their novels that would allow readers a fair chance of working out the guilty party. 'Do you promise', said one of the clauses in the club's membership ceremony, 'that your detectives shall well and truly detect the crimes presented to them, using those wits which it may please you to bestow upon them and not placing reliance upon nor making use of Divine Revelation, Feminine Intuition, Mumbo Jumbo, Jiggery Pokery, Coincidence, or any hitherto unknown Act of God?'

The rules were often breached but there was a genuine sense that the genre had conventions that needed to be observed. Tried and tested settings (the English country house, for example) appeared in dozens and dozens of novels in the 1930s. So too did stock characters – in some books it really was the butler who did it. At its worst, the supposed Golden Age produced a lot of tired, stale and cliché-ridden fiction. At its best – in the works of Christie, Sayers, Allingham, Marsh and others – it created sophisticated and witty narratives that have lost none of their entertainment value as the decades have passed.

## FROM THE DRAWING ROOM TO THE MEAN STREETS

Across the Atlantic, there were writers who were happy to produce their own American versions of the mannered and often eccentric mysteries that were so popular in Britain. Beginning with *The Benson Murder Case* in 1926, S.S. Van Dine wrote a dozen novels featuring the dandified aesthete and man-about-Manhattan Philo Vance. Two cousins, Frederick Dannay and Manfred B. Lee, joined forces to create Ellery Queen, both the pseudonym under which they wrote and the detective who starred in their books.

Side by side with these, however, were the growing numbers of American writers who were creating an indigenous form of crime writing that owed nothing to models from across the Atlantic. Most of them appeared first in the pages of the so-called 'pulp' magazines, of which the most famous was *Black Mask*, founded in 1920 by H.L. Mencken and George Jean Nathan but edited during its most influential years, the late 1920s and early 1930s, by Joseph Shaw. Carroll John Daly's two characters, Terry Mack and Race Williams, who appeared in *Black Mask* in 1923, were arguably the first hard-boiled sleuths of all. The star of the magazine, however, was » Dashiell Hammett. In a 1927 editorial, Joseph Shaw wrote that, 'Detective fiction as we see it has only commenced to be developed. All other fields have been worked and overworked, but detective fiction has barely been scratched.' It was Hammett who proved Shaw right. It was Hammett who, in the words of » Raymond Chandler, 'gave murder back to the people who commit it for reasons, not just to provide a corpse and with means at hand, not with hand-wrought dueling pistols, curare, and tropical fish.' Chandler himself, probably the most influential of all American crime writers, published his first story in *Black Mask* in 1933.

In some ways these two main strands of crime fiction – the elaborate puzzles of the classic English detective story and the hard-boiled crime that developed in the pulp magazines – have continued to this day. There have been many crossovers and many novelists who have successfully used elements of both but there is a tradition that links Christie and

Marsh with writers like **»** P.D. James and **»** Ruth Rendell just as there is a line that can be drawn from Hammett and Chandler to modern American novelists such as **»** James Ellroy and **»** Elmore Leonard.

## PICKING UP THE BATON

In England after the Second World War, the conventions of the Golden Age might have been thought to have become passé but they proved surprisingly resilient. Partly, of course, this was because the leading practitioners were still going strong. Sayers had put aside Lord Peter Wimsey in the late 1930s but Agatha Christie continued to publish fiction into the 1970s. Ngaio Marsh's last novel was published in 1982, **»** Gladys Mitchell's in 1984. Partly, it was because new writers arrived to revitalize the traditional form. **»** Edmund Crispin's first novels, featuring Gervase Fen, one of the great 'English eccentric' detectives, appeared in the late 1940s. **»** Michael Innes's earliest Inspector Appleby novels had been published in the late 1930s but he produced many more in later decades. **»** Michael Gilbert and **»** Julian Symons both began their careers as crime novelists immediately after the war. In the late 1960s and early 1970s, when the greatest practitioners of the Golden Age were coming to the ends of their careers, a third generation of writers emerged. P.D. James created the poet and policeman Adam Dalgleish; Ruth Rendell invented the Sussex town of Kingsmarkham in which Inspector Wexford could display his humane skills as a detective. New Queens of Crime had appeared on the scene.

In America after the war, writers emerged to pick up the baton from Hammett and Chandler. Kenneth Millar, using the pseudonym of **»** Ross Macdonald, created in Lew Archer a detective to rival Chandler's Philip Marlowe. The first Archer novel, *The Moving Target*, was published in

1949. In the 1950s, another important subgenre in American crime fiction came to the fore. Earlier novels like Lawrence Treat's *V for Victim* (1945) and Hillary Waugh's *Last Seen Wearing* (1952) can be claimed as pioneering police procedurals, but the type of crime fiction which attempts to show realistically the unfolding of a police investigation into a crime or crimes really came into its own with the publication of **»** Ed McBain's 87th Precinct books. Beginning with *Cop Hater* in 1956, McBain wrote dozens of these novels, set in a fictional city based on New York. The disclaimer that he placed at the beginning of each of them succinctly sums up his aim of blending reality and fiction. 'The city in these pages is imaginary. The people, the places are all fictitious. Only the police routine is based on established investigatory technique.'

Where McBain went in the 1950s, dozens of others have followed in the decades since. Indeed, the police procedural has become one of the most popular forms of crime fiction in all media. Not only novels but films and TV series show McBain's influence. It is hard to imagine a pioneering series like *Hill Street Blues*, for example, and all its imitators without the 87th Precinct.

## EXPLORING THE WHYS AND HOWS

There are other strands in crime fiction beyond those of classic English mystery and hard-boiled American realism. There is what is usually termed the psychological thriller which began in the 1930s and can be traced back to the novels Anthony Berkeley Cox wrote under the pseudonym of **»** Francis Iles. Here the emphasis is not on the solution of a puzzle (in Iles's *Malice Aforethought* there is no doubt who committed the murder) nor on the gritty realism of city life. The interest of the books lies in the slow unravelling of the psyche of the protagonist(s). Many of the finest writers in the genre, from » Patricia Highsmith and » Margaret Millar to » Barbara Vine and » Minette Walters, have chosen to work with the psychological thriller.

In another vein, there is the courtroom drama, which contemporary writers such as Scott Turow have made their own. Researchers into the history of the English version of this subgenre could locate prototypes in novels by Dickens and Trollope (or even, if over-diligent, in Shakespeare's *The Merchant of Venice*) but the beginnings of the American courtroom drama are best sought in the work of » Erle Stanley Gardner. Gardner was one of the writers for *Black Mask* in the 1920s but his real success came with the creation of the brilliant lawyer Perry Mason. Judged solely by total worldwide sales of books over the years, Mason is the second most popular character in crime fiction (only Sherlock Holmes outranks him) and his influence has been enormous. Beneath all the contemporary glitz and the plots expanded to fill narratives of blockbusting size, the characters in modern courtroom dramas by the likes of Turow and others are basically Perry Mason with attitude.

The forensic thriller has become increasingly popular in the last decade. Variants on the police procedural, where the emphasis is not on the cop on the beat but on the scientist in the laboratory, forensic thrillers found their doyenne in » Patricia Cornwell, whose success paved the way for many other fine writers, from Kathy Reichs to Karin Slaughter. With the remarkable popularity of TV series like the CSI franchise, this subgenre has spread from the printed page to other media until it has become one of the most visible of all forms of crime fiction.

Other subgenres can be readily identified (the black farce and comic capers of American writers from » Donald E. Westlake to » Carl Hiaasen;

the historical detective fiction that has proved so popular in both America and the UK) but the significance lies not in the number that can be formally anatomized but in what their variety says about the state of crime fiction today. Since the 1970s, the two major branches of the genre (broadly speaking, English cosy and American hard-boiled) have divided and proliferated to such an extent that the sheer range and quality of writing that gets shelved in bookshops and libraries under the heading of 'crime fiction' is remarkable. What other area of fiction in the last thirty years can offer such diverseness? From the tartan noir of **»** Ian Rankin to the Roman scandals of **»** Steven Saylor, from **»** Donna Leon's shadow-filled Venice to the mean streets of **»** Walter Mosley's LA, crime novels range through time and across the world to give readers a variety of experiences that no other style of fiction can match. Today, writers like **»** Daniel Woodrell and **»** Sue Grafton, **»** Michael Dibdin and **»** Tony Hillerman, **»** K.C. Constantine and Minette Walters have very little in common with one another except for the fact that they are all, in very different ways, fine novelists and they are all classified as crime writers.

So, this is the territory that this guide takes. There are adjoining lands (that of the spy thriller, for instance, or the blockbusting narratives of writers like John Grisham and Tom Clancy) that we could have visited but we have chosen to remain within the traditional boundaries of the crime genre. (Perhaps another book beckons in which the pure thriller, in all its many incarnations, can be explored.) We have tried to make our choice of 100 books as interesting and wide-ranging as possible. We have included classics from the genre's past like **»** John Dickson Carr's *The Hollow Man* and **»** Nicholas Blake's *The Beast Must Die*; we have drawn attention to rewardingly offbeat novels such as **»** Cameron McCabe's *The Face on the Cutting Room Floor* and **»** John Franklin

Bardin's *The Deadly Percheron*; and we have had to choose one particular title to represent such popular and prolific crime writers as » Lawrence Block, » Dick Francis, Erle Stanley Gardner, Patricia Highsmith, » John D. MacDonald and Ruth Rendell. In such a rich field of writing, the list of 100 we have compiled cannot hope or pretend to be a definitive one but it is one that has been great fun to select. We hope that readers will find books in it, both old favourites and new suggestions, that are just as much to fun to read.

Richard Shephard and Nick Rennison

2006

# A-ZOFENTRIES

## MARGERY ALLINGHAM (1905–66) UK

### THE TIGER IN THE SMOKE (1952)

Meg Elginbrodde, a young war widow, is the victim of a bizarre persecution which might or might not be the first move in a campaign of blackmail. Someone is sending her photographs which appear to show that her husband is still alive and well. Meanwhile the chilling and ruthless killer Jack Havoc has escaped from incarceration and is loose in the fog-shrouded streets of London. A bizarre band of beggars and con-artists led by one Tiddy Doll and the parishioners of the little city church of St Peter of the Gate both have reason to fear that Havoc, in search of revenge and a mysterious treasure he longs to possess, will descend upon them. As Allingham's plot unfolds, the two apparently disconnected stories of the widow and the murderer draw closer together and come to a climax in a nerve-racking encounter in a remote French village.

Allingham was one of the indisputably great writers of the so-called Golden Age of English detective fiction and her most famous creation, the affable and gentlemanly Albert Campion, is one of the most engaging of all amateur detectives of the period. She was a versatile writer and Campion was a flexible character, as much at home in stories of fast and furious farce as he was in more traditional mysteries and adventures. Although Campion plays an almost peripheral role in it, *The Tiger in the*

*Smoke* is Allingham's finest novel, a gripping narrative played out in the faded squares, dark alleys and shabby pubs of a long-vanished London. 'Dickensian' is an over-used adjective but many of the characters in the post-Second World War London she creates so brilliantly – from Jack Havoc himself to the sinister albino Tiddy Doll and the saintly Canon Avril – could indeed have stepped from the nineteenth-century city depicted in Dickens's novels.

 **Film version:** *Tiger in the Smoke* (1956)

 **Read on**

*Death of a Ghost*; *More Work for the Undertaker*; *Traitor's Purse*
**»** Edmund Crispin, *The Case of the Gilded Fly*; **»** Ngaio Marsh, *Surfeit of Lampreys*; **»** Dorothy L. Sayers, *Murder Must Advertise*

# ERIC AMBLER (1909–98) UK

## THE MASK OF DIMITRIOS (1939)

A prolific author and scriptwriter, Eric Ambler began writing fiction in 1936, after first trying his hand as a playwright. He had already written four acclaimed novels when, in 1939, the year heralding the advent of war, *The Mask of Dimitrios* appeared and was swiftly hailed as a classic spy story. Famously lauded by Graham Greene as being 'unquestionably our finest thriller writer', Ambler was a highly intelligent craftsman and virtually all his books benefited from his penchant for authoritative political backgrounds and a cool, detached style that was, and remains, extremely readable. With their dispassionate, left-leaning approach and subtle characterization, they were poles apart from the run-of-the-mill, imperialist yarns favoured by such writers as John Buchan and Sapper. Like the majority of his other works, *The Mask of Dimitrios* eschews the use of anything so vulgar as a hero and features as its protagonist a relatively normal and nondescript Englishman, Charles Latimer, a detective novelist and former academic, who is on holiday in Turkey. Prompted by a Turkish police chief who asks him, condescendingly, if he has any real experience of murder, he is gradually drawn into a complex and increasingly deadly international intrigue, centred on the apparent death of Dimitrios Makropolous, a notorious spy, trafficker and suspected murderer.

While Latimer probes the countries and associates connected with the enigmatic villain's nefarious activities, Ambler deftly reveals tantalizing snippets of the spy's very shady background, masterfully racking up the tension and suspense as Latimer draws ever closer to his supposedly deceased nemesis. Filmed in 1944, this powerful novel has since become a classic of the genre and, with its sombre and gripping depiction of dark political movements in 1930s' Europe, still has considerable relevance in today's uncertain global climate.

**&#128228; Film version:** *The Mask of Dimitrios* (1944)

## &#128218; Read on

*Epitaph for a Spy*; *Journey into Fear*; *Judgement on Deltchev*
Lionel Davidson, *The Night of Wenceslas*; Graham Greene, *Stamboul Train*; Geoffrey Household, *Rogue Male*

# JOHN FRANKLIN BARDIN (1916–81) USA

## THE DEADLY PERCHERON (1946)

John Franklin Bardin published nearly all his crime fiction in a short burst of creativity in the late 1940s and early 1950s and his novels are among the most startling and unusual ever produced by an American crime writer. They begin by establishing strange, almost surrealist scenarios which are gradually made explicable and rational as the plot develops. The explanations are not always entirely convincing but the hallucinatory oddness of the events which Bardin first establishes gives his fiction a memorable uniqueness.

*The Deadly Percheron*, his first book, begins in a psychiatrist's office where Dr George Matthews has a patient to see. The patient, who appears in most ways to be perfectly sane, has the strangest of stories to tell. He is employed by a group of little men, 'leprechauns', to wander the city streets and perform such unusual tasks as wearing flowers in his hair and handing out small change to passers by. His latest job is to deliver a heavy horse, a percheron, to the apartment of a well-known actress. Unsurprisingly, Matthews assumes that his patient is delusional but he is forced to reconsider when he gets to meet one of the 'leprechauns' himself. When the actress is murdered, he is obliged to take his patient's story even more seriously. As the bizarre plot unfolds, Matthews is attacked and wakes up in the city hospital where everyone believes him to be not an eminent psychiatrist but a deranged vagrant. He must slowly remember what has happened to him and gradually piece together the real story behind the weird events in which he has become embroiled. No précis can do justice to the baffling oddity of Bardin's plots. No other writer of crime stories is quite like him and his short, compelling novels should be read by all those who like their mystery novels to be so mysterious as to defy even the most ingenious, commonsensical attempts to explain them.

### ⋑ Read on

*Devil Take the Blue-Tail Fly; A Shroud for Grandmama*

# E.C. BENTLEY (1875–1956) UK

## TRENT'S LAST CASE (1913)

A lifelong friend of » G.K. Chesterton and best known for his invention of the four-line verse form the clerihew (the word derives from his middle name), Bentley earned his living as a journalist on *The Daily Telegraph*. He began *Trent's Last Case*, which is dedicated to Chesterton, as a spoof of the crime fiction of his day but it developed into a genuinely intriguing and satisfying mystery story. Set in an upper middle-class semi-bohemia which has long since disappeared, the book begins when American financier Sigsbee Manderson is found murdered and minus his false teeth in the garden of his English country home. Philip Trent is a languidly witty painter-about-town who decides that it is up to him to solve the mystery surrounding the American's death. He does everything that the amateur detective in such novels is supposed to do, painstakingly gathering evidence and assessing other characters' potential for murder, but he draws all the wrong conclusions. Clues are misinterpreted; suspicions fall on the wrong people. Trent also makes the cardinal mistake for any detective of falling in love with the chief suspect, Manderson's young, attractive and insufficiently grieving widow.

Trent is an engaging hero, if not a very effective one. (Only when the real criminal explains the sequence of events to him does he understand just how Manderson died.) He appeared only in this novel, in a collection of short stories (*Trent Intervenes*) and in a much less satisfying, longer narrative co-written with H. Warner Allen. Bentley may have intended his book as a pastiche of a genre that was growing ever more popular at the time it was published but it is as ingeniously plotted as any other mystery of the period and can now be read with pleasure as a perfect example of the kind of fiction it was originally meant to parody.

◀ **Film version:** *Trent's Last Case* (1952)

**☙ Read on**
*Trent Intervenes*
Anthony Berkeley, *The Silk Stocking Murders*; Ronald Knox, *The Footsteps at the Lock*

# NICHOLAS BLAKE (1904–72) Ireland

## THE BEAST MUST DIE (1938)

Frank Cairnes's son has been killed in a hit-and-run accident. Consumed by grief and guilt (should he have allowed his son to play in the village street as he did?), he becomes obsessed with tracking down the driver who hit the child and then callously drove on. Eventually, he believes he has found him. Adopting a new persona, he talks his way into the household of the guilty man, an unpleasant suburban bully named George Rattery, and begins to plan his murder. All seems to go wrong and Cairnes is obliged to shelve his plans – but Rattery is none the less found dead. When Cairnes's diary, detailing his plotting, comes to light, he becomes, unsurprisingly, the chief suspect and he is forced to call upon the services of Nigel Strangeways, the amateur detective who features in most of Nicholas Blake's mystery novels. Strangeways gradually draws nearer and nearer to the truth about a Machiavellian attempt to manipulate reality.

Nicholas Blake was the pseudonym of the poet and critic Cecil Day-Lewis and, under that name, he wrote detective stories from the 1930s, when his name was linked with W.H. Auden and other young left-wing writers of the day, to the 1960s, when he was appointed Poet Laureate in succession to John Masefield. All of them are witty, well written and deviously plotted but *The Beast Must Die* is the one that most skilfully combines a twisting and turning narrative with a subtle but unobtrusive study of the nature of private and public morality. Frank Cairnes's realization that the police and the authorities have failed him and that his only alternative is to pursue his own personal justice is sympathetically portrayed and readers are pulled in to the plot to murder Rattery that leads inexorably towards a denouement that even Cairnes did not imagine.

🎞 **Film version:** *Que La Bête Meure* (1969)

**≋ Read on**

*The Case of the Abominable Snowman*; *The Smiler With the Knife*
**»** Cyril Hare, *An English Murder*; **»** Michael Innes, *The Weight of the Evidence*; Philip MacDonald, *Murder Gone Mad*

# LAWRENCE BLOCK (b. 1938) USA

## WHEN THE SACRED GINMILL CLOSES (1986)

Block has been writing for over forty years and has produced more than sixty books, including three different series of novels and several volumes of stories. A versatile writer of almost limitless gifts, he is a consistently inventive plotter, possessed of a powerful imagination, a genial sense of humour and a willingness to explore the darker recesses of the human condition. Of all his books, arguably his most significant work has been the series of Matt Scudder novels, which, so far, numbers sixteen. The first few were written in the early seventies and began appearing in 1976, published as paperback originals. Set in the mean streets of a vividly depicted New York, they feature the compelling adventures and exploits of Scudder, an alcoholic, guilt-ridden ex-cop and unlicensed private investigator. Published in 1986, and with its title taken from a song by the folk singer and Bob Dylan mentor, Dave Van Ronk, *When the Sacred Ginmill Closes* is a key work in the Scudder cycle. As this same title suggests, it sees the ever-bibulous investigator finally resolve to keep his demons at bay with nothing stronger than black coffee, as he decides to give up drinking for good. The book's importance is heightened by the fact that it is actually a prequel, with Scudder recollecting various grim events that took place in the mid-seventies, but from the safe (and sober) perspective of a decade later. Corralled by his erstwhile drinking buddies into participating in some very dirty doings, involving blackmail and murder, and reinforced by a perpetual and heroic administering of Dutch courage, Scudder acquits himself well, with honour and liver more or less intact. Intriguingly, the author himself has suggested that readers approaching the series for the first time might begin with this volume, perhaps the highest recommendation of all.

### ⮜ Read on

*A Dance at the Slaughterhouse*; *Eight Million Ways to Die*; *A Walk Among the Tombstones* (all Matt Scudder novels); *The Burglar Who Thought He Was Bogart* (one of the best of Block's light-hearted series featuring the bookseller and burglar Bernie Rhodenbarr); *The Thief Who Couldn't Sleep*

» Michael Connelly, *A Darkness More Than Night*; Jonathan Valin, *Extenuating Circumstances*

# FREDRIC BROWN (1906–72) USA

## THE FABULOUS CLIPJOINT (1947)

A wildly inventive writer, Brown was equally at home in both crime and science fiction genres, successfully contrasting the former's gritty realism with the playful fantasies of the latter. Highly prolific, he wrote, alongside his novels, over three hundred stories for the pulp magazines – again, in both genres – beginning in 1936, when he was thirty years old and working as a journalist and proofreader. After eleven years, he produced his debut novel, *The Fabulous Clipjoint*, which won the Edgar Award for best first novel in 1948 and remained the author's favourite among his 23 crime novels. Set in an atmospherically depicted Chicago, it reveals how eighteen-year-old Ed Hunter teams up with his uncle Ambrose, a pleasantly dissolute carnival worker, as they investigate the mystery of Ed's father's death, encountering murder, mayhem and a slew of scantily clad damsels. As much a rites of passage story as it is a mystery novel, this was the first of seven books featuring Ed and Am Hunter, and it remains the best, but of a pretty good bunch.

Over his 30-year career, Brown was as adept at assembling excellent hardboiled stories – that could have drunk in the same saloons as the classic 1930s Warner Brothers gangster pictures – as he was at knocking out co(s)mic extraterrestrial stuff such as *Martians, Go Home*, his 1955 yarn about pesky green-skinned invaders. Further evidence of Brown's humour is to be found in many of his other titles, which include *We All Killed Grandma*, *The Case of the Dancing Sandwiches*, *The Screaming Mimi* and *Mrs Murphy's Underpants*, as well as his shortest ever story, which reads 'The last man on Earth sat alone in a room. There was a knock on the door…'

## ⮂ Read on
*The Dead Ringer*; *Night of the Jabberwock*; *The Screaming Mimi* Norbert Davis, *The Mouse in the Mountain*; Jonathan Latimer, *Murder in the Madhouse*; **»** Charles Williams, *The Diamond Bikini*

# JAMES LEE BURKE (b. 1936) USA

## THE NEON RAIN (1987)

A writer of great skill and power, Burke has been a novelist for almost forty years, beginning in the late 1960s, after he returned from duty in Vietnam. He had written five acclaimed novels, including the Pulitzer-nominated *The Lost Get-Back Boogie*, before his first crime novel, *The Neon Rain*, appeared in 1987. Set in a brilliantly evoked New Orleans, the book introduced Dave Robicheaux, Vietnam vet, practising Catholic and alcoholic police detective. A Cajun who lives in a houseboat on the river and a maverick investigator whose struggle not to succumb to his weakness for alcohol is a potent portion of the drama in the series, Robicheaux is a charismatic and highly compelling character. Vivid and beautiful descriptive passages of the region's flora and fauna contrast strongly with sudden descents into mind-boggling violence, revealing how the sensual and idyllic setting of Louisiana is also an arena seething in brooding, primeval malevolence.

The novel opens with Robicheaux indulging in his favourite pastime of fishing and, while testing his rod in a backwoods bayou, he discovers a body in the water. The corpse is that of a prostitute and addict, and repeated warnings from both sides of the law to let this seemingly unimportant death be quietly filed away convince him that he is stumbled on to something nasty. Before long, he is mired in a swamp of corrupt police officials, local mobsters, Nicaraguan drug dealers, Treasury agents and retired military personnel, along with a scheme to smuggle arms to the Contras. As these disparate forces combine to first frame him and then kill him, he is soon trying desperately to stay one step ahead of his assailants and fighting for his life. Burke is one of the most important crime novelists to have emerged in the last twenty years, and this remains one of finest books.

### ⮑ Read on

*Black Cherry Blues*; *Heaven's Prisoners*; *In the Electric Mist With Confederate Dead*; *A Stained White Radiance* (all Dave Robicheaux novels); *Cimarron Rose*
» Robert Crais, *Voodoo River*; Tony Dunbar, *The Crooked Man*; » Dennis Lehane, *Mystic River*

# JAMES M. CAIN (1892–1977) USA

## DOUBLE INDEMNITY (1936)

Memorably, if prudishly, described as 'a Proust in greasy overalls, a dirty little boy with a piece of chalk and a board fence and nobody watching', by fellow crime novelist » Raymond Chandler, Cain had already written his first hardboiled classic, *The Postman Always Rings Twice* (1933) and was ensconced as a scriptwriter in Hollywood when his second book, *Double Indemnity*, became a bestseller in 1936. Others disagreed with Chandler, such as critic Edmund Wilson, who shrewdly lauded Cain as 'a poet of the tabloid murder'. A powerful, though limited writer, Cain had no qualms about writing about sex and most of his books have a common theme – that of sexual obsession and temptation leading an ordinary, but weak, man to commit evil and, ultimately, to pay for it. The majority of his best work appeared in the 1930s – the Depression years – and his torrid tales concerning the lure of dollars and desire proved irresistible to millions of Americans weary of being told to tighten their belts and keep them done up. It also touched a chord with French intellectuals, who recognized Cain's gritty, earthy realism as a prototype of existentialism.

*Double Indemnity* tells the story of insurance salesman, Walter Huff, who is helplessly entranced by the saucy and seductive siren, Phyllis Nirdlinger, and cooks up a scam whereby they'll kill her husband, make it look like an accident and clean up on his life assurance policy. All they have to do is not arouse the suspicions of the police, the insurance company, the sexy stepdaughter, Lola, or her disaffected boyfriend, and, naturally, keep their hands from one another's throats. This scorching crime classic was the basis for Billy Wilder's movie of the same name, a smash hit that ushered in *film noir* and was, ironically, co-scripted by Chandler himself.

**Film version:** *Double Indemnity* (1944)

## Read on

*The Butterfly*; *Mildred Pierce*; *The Postman Always Rings Twice*; *Serenade*

W.R. Burnett, *The Asphalt Jungle*; Horace McCoy, *No Pockets in a Shroud*; » Charles Williams, *Hell Hath No Fury* (aka *The Hot Spot*)

# PAUL CAIN (1902–66) USA

## FAST ONE (1933)

An enigmatic figure, Cain was born George Sims in Iowa, and grew up in Chicago. He moved to Los Angeles aged eighteen and became a scriptwriter, but little else is known of his early life, making his exotic account of travelling the world as a bosun's mate, Dadaist painter and professional gambler impossible to verify. In 1932, as Paul Cain, he submitted a story to the famous crime magazine, *Black Mask* and, after writing a further four stories, put these together to produce his only novel, the extraordinary *Fast One*. Praised by **»** Raymond Chandler as 'some kind of high point in the ultra hardboiled manner', *Fast One* is an absolute classic, with its frenzied action depicted in staccato prose. Gunman, gambler and big drinker Gerry Kells arrives in 1930s Los Angeles with $2,000 and a reputation as a very tough guy. As he muscles his way into the LA rackets, he teams up with the beautiful, equally bibulous S. Grandquist, her past as mysterious as her first name, and together they take on rival gangs, before bringing down the curtain in a booze-fuelled explosion of violence and death.

After penning stories for other pulp magazines, as well as several more for *Black Mask*, some of which were subsequently collected and published in 1946 as *Seven Slayers* (his only other book), Cain returned to writing screenplays under the name Peter Ruric. These included scripts for *The Black Cat*, directed by B-movie maestro Edgar G. Ulmer and starring Boris Karloff and Bela Lugosi, and *Mademoiselle Fifi*, adapted from two Guy de Maupassant stories and produced by Val Lewton, the man behind *Cat People* and other low budget chillers. Cain wrote articles and television scripts before succumbing to cancer in 1966, but never again produced anything as powerful as *Fast One*.

### ≋ Read on

*Seven Slayers*

» Raymond Chandler, *Trouble is My Business*; » Dashiell Hammett, *The Big Knockover*, *Red Harvest*; Roger Torrey, *42 Days for Murder*

## JOHN DICKSON CARR (1906–77) USA

### THE HOLLOW MAN (1935)

John Dickson Carr was an Anglophile American writer whose books are most often set in the kind of fantasy England that never really existed outside the imagination of Anglophile Americans. His speciality as a crime novelist was the 'locked room mystery' and *The Hollow Man*, published in the USA as *The Three Coffins*, is probably the cleverest of all his stories. Featuring his series character Dr Gideon Fell, a scholarly eccentric with a love of good food, fine wine and improbable crimes who was supposedly modelled on » G.K. Chesterton, the book opens with the gathering of Professor Grimaud and a small group of his learned and literary friends in a Bloomsbury tavern. Into their midst comes a gaunt and shabby man in black who talks mysteriously of a man who can get up out of his coffin and can move anywhere invisibly and who makes vague threats of what he and a brother he can summon to assist him will do to Grimaud. Grimaud laughs off the man's threats but a few nights later the professor is found murdered. His killer apparently walked through a locked door, shot him and then vanished into thin air. A second victim of the same, seemingly diabolical murderer is shot in the middle of an empty, snow-covered street which is under observation from both ends. No one is seen and no footprints are left in the snow. Carr sets his scene with great efficiency in the first few chapters of his book and then spends the rest of it slowly unveiling, with monumental ingenuity, the logic behind the seemingly illogical events. Even more strongly than any of his other novels, *The Hollow Man* draws readers inexorably into its fantastic plot, baffling and flummoxing them until Gideon Fell finally explains all and brings the events back into the realm of the rational.

## ⮒ Read on

*The Crooked Hinge* (another story in which Fell investigates a seemingly impossible murder); *Hag's Nook*; *The White Priory Murders* (one of the best of the series of novels which Carr wrote under the alias of Carter Dickson and which featured the eccentric and self-indulgent barrister and sleuth Sir Henry Merrivale)

Anthony Boucher, *The Case of the Locked Key*; » Edmund Crispin, *Holy Disorders*; Ellery Queen, *The Chinese Orange Mystery*

## READONATHEME: LOCKED ROOM MYSTERIES

Catherine Aird, *His Burial Too*
» Margery Allingham, *Flowers for the Judge*
» Agatha Christie, *Hercule Poirot's Christmas*
Freeman Wills Crofts, *The End of Andrew Harrison*
» Carter Dickson (John Dickson Carr), *The Cavalier's Cup*
» Edgar Allan Poe, *The Murders in the Rue Morgue* (the short story that is the grandfather of all locked room mysteries)
Bill Pronzini, *Hoodwink*
Clayton Rawson, *Death From a Top Hat*
Maj Sjöwall and Per Wahlöö, *The Locked Room*
Israel Zangwill, *The Big Bow Mystery*

# VERA CASPARY (1899–87) USA

## LAURA (1943)

A name rarely found in crime anthologies, Vera Caspary was an acclaimed author of stories and novels, and also wrote, or co-wrote, a number of successful Broadway plays and numerous screenplays. Among her many mystery novels, two of them, *Laura* (1943) and *Bedelia*, written two years later, are considered to be classics and were both filmed successfully. Set in the sophisticated high-ish society of 1940s' Manhattan, *Laura* opens with police detective Mark McPherson investigating the murder of Laura

Hunt, a beautiful, intelligent and ambitious young advertising executive, who was due to marry her fiancé, Shelby Carpenter, in a few days. With her playwright's skill, Caspary deftly assembles an intriguing and eccentric cast, including assorted arrogant friends, the handsome but vacuous Carpenter and Laura's friend and mentor, celebrated columnist Waldo Lydecker, for whom the term 'waspish' might well have been coined. Smitten with his protégé, the wily Lydecker has for years been using his column to ridicule and thereby eliminate Laura's gentlemen friends, with only Carpenter seemingly immune to his vitriolic barbs. Gradually, McPherson (and the reader) gets to know the real Laura and, her demise notwithstanding, begins to fall for her, even as he ponders how such a lovely, sensitive creature could have kept company with a coterie of hedonistic poseurs and parasites. With a brilliant and entirely credible twist, however, Caspary turns McPherson – and the whole story, in fact – upside down, giving the book a whole new direction. Despite being frequently praised as a *noir* novel, it does not really fit into that category, although the policeman's growing romantic obsession with a corpse and the fatal shotgun blast to the face certainly provide the novel with a substantial edge, but it remains a uniquely powerful and mesmerizing novel, and a high point in Caspary's successful career.

📽 **Film version:** *Laura* (1944)

🔖 **Read on**

*Bedelia*

Leigh Brackett, *No Good From a Corpse*; Dorothy B. Hughes, *In a Lonely Place*; Hilda Lawrence, *Death of a Doll*; Evelyn Piper, *Bunny Lake is Missing*

# RAYMOND CHANDLER (1888–1959) USA

## THE BIG SLEEP (1939)

This was the first novel by the man widely praised as the poet of the hardboiled school of crime writing, and was written after Chandler had served his apprenticeship, having spent six years writing, with increasing skill and success, crime stories for the popular pulp magazine *Black Mask*. Cannibalized, as his early novels often were, from two of these pulp stories, *The Big Sleep* shows, however, that the extended format suited Chandler fine; he had room to manoeuvre, to add several touches of class and his own brand of magic, and, as he put it, to 'go a bit further, be a bit more humane, get a bit more interested in people than in violent death'.

*The Big Sleep* introduced the reader to private investigator Philip Marlowe, hero of all Chandler's novels and an iconic creation in crime fiction and *noir* cinema, a knight errant who is poor, but scrupulously honest, an anomaly in the corrupt and venal world of 1930s' and '40s' Los Angeles, 'the neon-lighted slum' that is the setting for the books. The plot, never the strongest or most important element in Chandler's fiction, revolves around Marlowe's search for a millionaire's missing son-in-law, and his encounters with the wealthy man's two beautiful daughters; one married to the missing man, but less keen on finding him once she sees Marlowe, and the other an erotic little lunatic. Tough, handy with a gun, but handier with a wisecrack, Marlowe is soon up to his neck in blackmail, drugs and murder, desperately trying to solve a mystery that swiftly becomes complex and convoluted, its twists and turns punctuated by a growing number of corpses. Filmed several times, *The Big Sleep* soon became an absolute classic of crime fiction and paved the way for Chandler's literary immortality.

◤ **Film versions:** *The Big Sleep* (1946); *The Big Sleep* (1978)

## ❧ Read on
*The Long Goodbye*; *The High Window*
Howard Browne, *The Taste of Ashes*; » Dashiell Hammett, *The Maltese Falcon*; » Ross Macdonald, *The Moving Target*

## FAREWELL, MY LOVELY (1940)
Opening with an encounter between Philip Marlowe and one of Chandler's most memorable characters, the man-mountain Moose Malloy, *Farewell, My Lovely* develops into a hectic rollercoaster ride through a southern California peopled by a gallery of grotesques, from the sinister psychic Jules Amthor to the drunkenly flirtatious Mrs Florian. Marlowe just happens to be passing when the giant Malloy, recently released from prison and 'about as inconspicuous as a tarantula on a slice of angel food', arrives at a black club where his girlfriend Velma used to work. Moose wants to see little Velma again and he is not going to listen to claims from the current club manager that he does not know where she is. In the course of interrogating the unfortunate manager, who truly does not know anything about Velma, Moose inadvertently kills him and exits stage left. Intrigued, Marlowe begins his own enquiries into the missing woman's whereabouts. Another case, in which the private eye is asked to assist in the handing over of a ransom for a valuable piece of jewellery, turns out to be closely connected with Velma's disappearance. As he pursues the truth, Marlowe is subjected to a series of beatings, doped to the eyeballs and imprisoned in an illegally run sanatorium, and threatened by cops and criminals alike but still succeeds in revealing what has really become of Velma. However,

the revelation brings little but death and disaster to everyone, from Velma herself to the giant, lovelorn Moose. Chandler's second novel, often claimed to be his own favourite among his books, is a masterpiece of *noir* fiction. Told in the unmistakeable, wisecracking voice of Philip Marlowe, it is filled with breathless action and memorable dialogue. And, beneath all the richness and humour of Chandler's prose, there is a melancholy and romantic story of archetypal American dreams crumbling to dust under the unforgiving Los Angeles sun.

**Film versions:** *Farewell, My Lovely* (US: *Murder, My Sweet*) (1944); *Farewell, My Lovely* (1975)

## Read on
*The Lady in the Lake*; *The Little Sister*
Arthur Lyons, *Other People's Money*; » Walter Mosley, *Devil in a Blue Dress*; » Robert B. Parker, *Poodle Springs*

## READONATHEME: CLASSIC PRIVATE EYES PAST AND PRESENT

Max Allan Collins, *True Detective* (Nate Heller)
Howard Engel, *A City Called July* (Benny Cooperman)
Stephen Greenleaf, *Past Tense* (John Marshall Tanner)
» Dashiell Hammett, *The Maltese Falcon* (Sam Spade)
Jeremiah Healy, *The Staked Goat* (John Francis Cuddy)
Michael Z. Lewin, *Called by a Panther* (Albert Samson)

Arthur Lyons, *False Pretences* (Jacob Asch)
» Ross Macdonald, *The Underground Man* (Lew Archer)
» Walter Mosley, *A Little Yellow Dog* (Easy Rawlins)
» George Pelecanos, *Down by the River Where the Dead Men Go* (Nick Stefanos)
Bill Pronzini, *Scattershot* (Nameless)
Jonathan Valin, *Missing* (Harry Stoner)

## JAMES HADLEY CHASE (1906–85) UK

### NO ORCHIDS FOR MISS BLANDISH (1939)

James Hadley Chase was just one of the pseudonyms used by London-born Réné Brabazon Raymond, a former salesman of children's encyclo-paedias, who started writing after reading American hardboiled pulp fiction. He wrote over forty thrillers and gangster stories, at least twenty of which were filmed. Although they are set mainly in America, he only paid the country two brief visits, to Florida and New Orleans, relying instead on maps and slang dictionaries.

Chase's first novel, *No Orchids for Miss Blandish*, was written over a period of six weekends in 1938, published the following year, as war was looming, and was an instant success, selling half a million copies over the next five years, during the wartime paper shortages; it was the book most widely read by British troops during the war. In 1944, George

Orwell wrote about it in an article, 'Raffles and Miss Blandish', in *Horizon* magazine, agreeing with the opinion expressed by some of his peers that it was 'pure Fascism', but also admitting that it was 'a brilliant piece of writing, with hardly a wasted word or a jarring note anywhere'. The novel's stage adaptation, co-scripted by Chase, Robert Nesbitt and Val Guest, ran from 1942 to 1949 and it was filmed – in America, but never in Britain – in 1948 and again in 1971, as *The Grissom Gang*, directed by Robert Aldrich. Borrowing its plot from William Faulkner's 1931 novel *Sanctuary*, it concerns the fate of the eponymous young heiress, who is abducted, held to ransom and raped by a vicious, depraved criminal, who is obsessed with and dominated by his mother, a lurid detail presaging James Cagney's Ma-fixated character, Cody Jarrett, in Raoul Walsh's 1949 film, *White Heat*. It was revised by Chase in 1961, with the slang updated and, since publication, has sold over two million copies.

**Film versions:** *No Orchids for Miss Blandish* (1948); *The Grissom Gang* (1971)

**Read on**
*This Way for a Shroud, Tiger by the Tail*
Peter Cheyney, *This Man is Dangerous* (one of a series by a British writer featuring Lemmy Caution, a hard-bitten New York G-man); William Faulkner, *Sanctuary*; W.L. Heath, *Violent Saturday*; » Mickey Spillane, *My Gun is Quick*

# G.K. CHESTERTON (1874–1936) UK

## THE INNOCENCE OF FATHER BROWN (1911)

G.K. Chesterton was a writer of many talents who published dozens of books in his lifetime on subjects ranging from theology to literary criticism. His place in the history of crime fiction was won by his creation of the unassuming Catholic priest Father Brown, forever alert to the frailties of human nature, who featured in a series of short stories which showcased Chesterton's gift for paradox and his ingenuity in creating both puzzles and their solutions. Many of the best stories appeared in the volume entitled *The Innocence of Father Brown*. Father Brown and his friend, the thief turned private investigator Flambeau, pursue a murderer who appears to have the power of invisibility, coming and going and leaving footsteps in the snow without anyone observing him. The priest solves another murder after realizing that the supposed suicide note the victim left is the 'wrong' shape. Brown, with a little help from Flambeau, works out how a man committed murder when a hundred people saw him practising his religious rites at the exact time his lover fell to her death. Chesterton sets up the puzzling scenarios in his stories with great skill and then allows Father Brown to reveal the solutions with impeccable, if ingenious, logic and insight.

In any other detective stories the flamboyant Flambeau, a great creation in his own right, would take centre stage but, in Chesterton's narratives, he plays second fiddle to the modest priest with the gift for imagining himself in the position of the criminal. 'Are you a devil?' the murderer in one story asks when Father Brown seems to read his mind with ease. 'I am a man,' the priest replies, 'and therefore have all devils in my heart.' It is his knowledge of the devils in his own heart and those of others that enables him to perform the apparently impossible feats of deduction which enliven Chesterton's wonderfully enjoyable short stories.

## ⮂ Read on

*The Wisdom of Father Brown*; *The Man Who Knew Too Much* (a collection of stories about another amateur detective, Horne Fisher)
R. Austin Freeman, *Dr Thorndyke's Casebook*; Baroness Orczy, *The Old Man in the Corner*; Edgar Wallace, *The Mind of Mr J.G. Reeder*

---

### READ ON A THEME: RELIGIOUS SLEUTHS

Margaret Coel, *The Dream Stalker* (Father John O'Malley)
Andrew Greeley, *The Bishop in the West Wing* (Bishop Blackie Ryan)
D.M. Greenwood, *Clerical Errors* (Deaconess Theodora Braithwaite)
Harry Kemelman, *Friday the Rabbi Slept Late* (Rabbi Small)
William X. Kienzle, *The Rosary Murders* (Father Robert Koesler)
Arturo Pérez-Reverte, *The Seville Communion* (Father Lorenzo Quart)
» Ellis Peters, *The Leper of St Giles* (Brother Cadfael)
Phil Rickman, *The Smile of a Ghost* (Reverend Merrily Watkins)
Peter Tremayne, *Absolution by Murder* (Sister Fidelma)

---

# AGATHA CHRISTIE (1890–1976) UK

## THE MURDER OF ROGER ACKROYD (1926)

This intricately plotted mystery is the best of the early novels to feature Christie's famous Belgian sleuth Hercule Poirot. Successful businessman turned country squire Roger Ackroyd lives in one of those archetypal English villages in which so many of Agatha Christie's narratives are set. As is always the case in her novels, dark secrets and dangerous emotions lurk beneath the apparently placid surface of village life. When Ackroyd is murdered, stabbed in the neck while sitting in his study after a dinner party, there are plenty of suspects, from his friend, the big game hunter Hector Blunt, to his adopted son, Ralph Paton and his niece Flora. Poirot, new neighbour to the narrator of the novel, the village physician, Dr Sheppard, is brought into the investigation of the murder and, after many twists and turns in the plot, is able to gather all the suspects together and reveal the extraordinary and unexpected identity of the killer.

It is easy to criticize Agatha Christie, and plenty of people over the decades have pointed out the woodenness of her characterization, the lack of credibility in much of her dialogue and the infelicities of her prose. None of this matters very much, if at all. She remains the supreme exponent of the old-fashioned English crime novel. Her skill in constructing complex and puzzling plots and her ability to deceive readers until the very last page (in some cases, the very last paragraph) of her stories are more than compensation for any shortcomings she might have as a writer. In the eighty years since the publication of *The Murder of Roger Ackroyd*, the ingenious twist on which the story hinges has been repeated in other novels by other writers but it retains much of the shock value for contemporary readers that it had in the 1920s.

## 🕮 Read on

*Death on the Nile*; *Murder in Mesopotamia*; *Murder on the Orient Express*
Christianna Brand, *Green for Danger*; Georgette Heyer, *Envious Casca*;
» Ngaio Marsh, *A Grave Mistake*

## A MURDER IS ANNOUNCED (1950)

In the village of Chipping Cleghorn, a bizarre entry is found amid the 'For Sale' notices and job advertisements in the personal column of the local paper. 'A murder is announced,' it reads, 'and will take place on Friday, October 29th, at Little Paddocks at 6.30 p.m.' Curious villagers are baffled. Is this a practical joke or an invitation to a murder game? At the appointed hour several of them do turn up at Little Paddocks, home of Letitia Blacklock, to await developments. Prompt at 6.30, the lights go out, a man, apparently clutching a revolver, shouts, 'Stick 'em up' in a voice reminiscent of American gangster films and shots ring out. When the lights go back on again, Miss Blacklock is found slightly wounded and the intruder is lying dead in the room. Detective Inspector Craddock, investigating the murder, discovers that most of the people gathered at Little Paddocks that evening have secrets to hide but he is powerless to prevent further killings in the village. Only Jane Marple, staying with the daughter of an old friend, wife of Chipping Cleghorn's vicar, is able eventually to reveal the truth behind the murder that was so brazenly announced before it happened.

Agatha Christie's second great creation, after Hercule Poirot, Miss Marple is seen at her best in this characteristically ingenious and engaging novel. Gently coaxing information from the villagers over cups of tea and cakes, the elderly spinster reveals her unexpected shrewdness about human nature and the passions that can possess the most unlikely individuals as she works her way quietly but inexorably towards a solution to the murderous events that have shattered Chipping Cleghorn's tranquillity. Miss Marple's 'little grey cells', as this novel shows better than any of the others in which she appears, are as powerfully effective as the ones on which Poirot so regularly prides himself.

### ⮑ Read on

*The Murder at the Vicarage* (the first of the twelve novels featuring Miss Marple); *The Moving Finger*; *The Mirror Crack'd From Side to Side*

M.C. Beaton, *Agatha Raisin and the Murderous Marriage*; Simon Brett, *A Nice Class of Corpse*; Patricia Wentworth, *Miss Silver Intervenes*

# HARLAN COBEN (b. 1962) USA

## TELL NO ONE (2001)

A writer who made his first appearance little over a decade ago, Coben is now one of the most consistently successful crime authors, with a dozen books and almost as many awards to his credit. Beginning in 1995 with *Deal Breaker*, he has published eight books in a series featuring Myron Bolitar, a former basketball player, forced out of the game due to injury, who now runs a sports agency. An extremely likeable character with a choice line in sharp, dry humour, Myron is smart, tender and tough if necessary, but really just wants to be a professional ballplayer again.

Coben then changed direction and has so far written five 'stand alone' novels, all highly successful. The first, *Tell No One*, begins with David and Elizabeth Beck, a young married couple who were childhood sweethearts, driving to Lake Charmaine, Pennsylvania. There, they'll celebrate the anniversary of their first kiss, taken when they were both twelve. The tryst is savagely interrupted when Elizabeth is abducted and murdered, while David is beaten and left for dead. Eight years later and David is now a practising paediatrician and, though his wife's killer is caught and tried, and he himself has physically recovered, he still grieves for Elizabeth. News that two eight-year-old-corpses have been found near the lake startles him, but even more astounding is an email arriving on the day of the anniversary of the attack, telling him to log on to a website at a specific time – the moment of that first kiss – and to use a code known only to him and Elizabeth. Other than that, there is a single command: tell no one. Coben masterfully piles on the suspense and tension, maintaining a relentless pace that holds till the final page, leaving the reader exalted, drained and desperate to tell everyone.

## ≋ Read on

*Back Spin*; *Darkest Fear*; *Deal Breaker*; *One False Move* (all Myron Bolitar novels)

» Robert Crais, *LA Requiem*; » Robert Ferrigno, *Heartbreaker*; T. Jefferson Parker, *California Girl*

# WILKIE COLLINS (1824–89) UK

## THE MOONSTONE (1868)

Often claimed by historians of the genre as the forerunner of all modern detective novels, *The Moonstone* is memorable for its elaborate narrative of intrigue, haunting and death and for the appearance of Sergeant Cuff, prototype of so many of the fictional policemen to come. It opens with a description of how a colonel in the British army desecrated a Hindu holy place during the siege of Seringapatam by stealing from it a fabulous diamond. The colonel leaves the jewel to his young niece, Rachel Verinder, and a gentleman named Franklin Blake travels to her Yorkshire home to present her with it as an eighteenth birthday present. On the eve of the birthday the fated diamond is once again stolen and Collins's story (told, like many of his novels, from a number of different perspectives) begins to unfold. Mysterious Hindus, exotic visitors to the Yorkshire countryside, are glimpsed in the neighbourhood; servants fall under suspicion as Cuff pursues his investigation into the theft; Franklin Blake falls under the dangerous spell of opium; and a pious hypocrite named Godfrey Ablewhite plots and schemes in the background. Eventually the truth emerges and the Moonstone returns to its rightful owners.

Wilkie Collins was a close friend of Dickens and master of what became known as 'sensation fiction', a school of Victorian fiction which came to the fore in the 1860s and which often took murder, mystery and crime as its subjects. His most famous novel, *The Woman in White*, published in 1860, is a melodramatic and complicated tale of a conspiracy to dispossess an heiress of her money, filled with dark secrets of lunacy, illegitimacy and mistaken identities, and made memorable by the suave and sinister Italian villain, Count Fosco. *The Moonstone*, published eight years later, is no less melodramatic but more clearly falls into the category of crime fiction and, nearly a century and a half after it first appeared, it retains its ability to intrigue and entertain readers.

◣ **Film versions:** *The Moonstone* (1934); *The Moonstone* (TV 1996)

⮾ **Read on**
*The Dead Secret*; *The Woman in White*
Mary Elizabeth Braddon, *Lady Audley's Secret* (another of the 'sensation' novels of the 1860s); Charles Dickens, *Bleak House*; » Fergus Hume, *Madame Midas*

# MICHAEL CONNELLY (b. 1956) USA

## THE BLACK ECHO (1992)
Unique in crime fiction for having created a character named after an enigmatic Flemish painter from the Middle Ages, Connelly has written, among additional books, nine novels featuring LAPD detective Hieronymus 'Harry' Bosch. Bursting on the scene in 1992 in *The Black Echo*, Bosch ticked most of the right boxes in that he was a Vietnam veteran, a disaffected loner and a single-minded maverick who often bucked the system and always got results. What made him different from scores of similar cynical sleuths were the occasional glimpses of

warmth visible under his stoic surface and his desire, perhaps compulsion, to 'speak for the dead', to seek and claim justice for the deceased. Raised mainly as an orphan, he spent some of his childhood in foster care after his mother was arrested for prostitution and later killed; a murder that he solved decades later. After service in Vietnam as a 'tunnel rat', he joined the police and eventually became a homicide detective. *The Black Echo* finds Bosch reliving some of his combat traumas when a body discovered in a Mulholland Dam drainpipe turns out to be that of Billy Meadows, a fellow tunnel rat who served alongside him, the two of them fighting their own stygian, subterranean war. As his investigation unfolds, he is soon pitted against departmental foes who want him quietly to drop the case, as well as against a gang of bold and ruthless crooks, intent on using Billy's underground experience for a heist. Bosch also encounters a beautiful and mysterious FBI agent, and together they struggle to crack the case, their initial differences ebbing as they begin to work well together and start to become interested in one another. Powerful, gripping and brimming with tension, *The Black Echo* is a superlative introduction to one of LA's finest cops, who remains an enduring hero in contemporary crime fiction.

## ⮂ Read on

*Angel's Flight*; *The Concrete Blonde*; *A Darkness More Than Night*; *Trunk Music* (all Harry Bosch novels); *The Poet*
Jeffery Deaver, ***The Bone Collector***; **»** James Ellroy, ***The Black Dahlia***

# K.C. CONSTANTINE (b. 1934) USA

## THE MAN WHO LIKED TO LOOK AT HIMSELF (1973)

An enigmatic writer, who rarely gives interviews and whose real name is even a matter of debate, K.C. Constantine is the creator of Mario Balzic, chief of police in the fictional Pennsylvania town of Rocksburg. Beginning with *The Rocksburg Railroad Murders* in 1972, he has written nearly twenty gritty novels which chronicle Balzic's life in a once-proud industrial town that is suffering from the effects of industrial decline. Men have lost their jobs and their self-respect. Old values and beliefs are under threat. Constantine uses the conventions and motifs of crime fiction to write novels in which these changes are brilliantly explored. Like » George V. Higgins, he is at his best in his dialogue, which shows he has a pitch-perfect ear for the rhythms and music of everyday American speech. In the second of the Rocksburg books, *The Man Who Liked to Look at Himself,* Constantine is in top form as Balzic painstakingly works towards the truth about a murder that only comes to light when an assortment of body parts is unearthed in land leased out for hunting. Amid controversies stirred by allegations of police racism and the distractions provided by over-eager subordinates, the police chief is determined to find the killer. As in all the Rocksburg novels, the crime becomes the hook on which Constantine can hang his analysis of the society in which it takes place.

In more recent novels such as *Blood Mud*, in which Balzic, retired but investigating dodgy insurance claims, is struggling with health problems, Constantine has very nearly deserted the crime genre altogether in favour of fiction driven entirely by character. Paradoxically, Balzic and his world seem less vivid in these later novels than they do in earlier books such as *The Man Who Liked to Look at Himself*, in which the dialogue and the characterization are more in service to a conventional crime plot.

## ⮂ Read on

*The Man Who Liked Slow Tomatoes*; *The Rocksburg Railroad Murders*
» George V. Higgins, *The Rat on Fire*


# PATRICIA CORNWELL (b. 1952) USA

## POSTMORTEM (1991)

Patricia Cornwell introduced her character Dr Kay Scarpetta, chief medical officer for the city of Richmond, Virginia, in this compelling story of a serial killer on the loose. A succession of women have been raped and murdered in their own homes. Theories about the killer proliferate but there is little real indication of who he is or how he chooses his victims. At the same time, someone is leaking information about the case to the press and it looks as if it comes from Scarpetta's office. Under pressure from her superiors, some of whom have never accustomed themselves to the idea of a woman in such a high-profile job, Scarpetta is determined to dig up new forensic evidence to nail the killer but her efforts seem likely to make her the next target.

As the Scarpetta series has progressed, characters have grown and developed, from the central character herself to her much-loved niece

Lucy (here seen as a precocious, ten-year-old computer whiz) and the bluntly down-to-earth police officer Pete Marino, but all the elements which have made Cornwell such a bestseller are already in place in this first book. Before she turned to writing, she worked in a crime lab and her insider's knowledge is clear in her detailed descriptions of the forensic investigations which lead Scarpetta towards the truth. Readers are invited to look over Scarpetta's shoulder as she marshals her evidence and it is the skilful combination of authentic science and tight plotting which provides the suspense and tension in Cornwell's novels. Many other novelists have followed her example by writing crime stories in which much of the fascination lies in the often gruesome details of the autopsy room and the forensic lab but few have been able either to create characters as complex and interesting as Scarpetta or to place them in plots which seize hold of readers with such a powerful grip.

### ⮒ Read on

*Body of Evidence*; *The Body Farm*; *From Potter's Field*
Tess Gerritsen, *The Surgeon*; Jonathan Kellerman, *Over the Edge*; Carol O'Connell, *Mallory's Oracle*; Kathy Reichs, *Déjà Dead*

# ROBERT CRAIS (b. 1953) USA

## THE MONKEY'S RAINCOAT (1987)
A former scriptwriter for such televisions shows as *Cagney & Lacey*, *Hill Street Blues* and *Miami Vice*, Crais has, like » Michael Connelly,

successfully made Los Angeles his literary stamping ground. Of his thirteen novels to date, ten have featured his private detective Elvis Cole, introduced in 1987 in *The Monkey's Raincoat*. An investigator in the classic mould, Cole is smart, wisecracking, cool and very tough. Like Michael Connelly's Harry Bosch, he is also a Vietnam veteran, but one who, on the surface, has a sunnier, more easy-going disposition, probably best summed up by the talismanic Pinocchio clock and Jiminy Cricket figurine adorning his office. He has a reasonably successful career as a private eye, in which he is aided by his friend and fellow veteran, the extremely taciturn and even tougher Joe Pike, who adds a whole new stratum of meaning to the expression 'silent partner'. Eyes masked by ubiquitous black shades, Pike is implacable, aloof and absolutely deadly; a sidekick more fascinating than most heroes and a man whom Cole would trust with his life.

In *The Monkey's Raincoat*, a pleasant woman named Ellen Lang hires Cole to track down her missing husband and young son. What starts out as a fairly simple case swiftly becomes increasingly complex and dangerous and, before long, he and Pike become embroiled in a deadly chase, one that takes them from some of LA's meaner streets to the beautiful boulevards paraded by the upper echelons of Hollywood's elite. Along the way, they uncover a murky melange of sex, drugs and murder, and the case concludes in something approaching a bloodbath, or, as an LAPD detective puts it, 'like Rambo Goes to Hollywood'. With this atmospheric, entertaining and hugely exciting novel, Crais inaugurated a wonderful series and, in Cole and Pike, he fashioned an inimitable team.

📚 **Read on**

*LA Requiem*; *Lullaby Town*; *Stalking the Angel*; *Sunset Express* (all Elvis Cole novels); *Demolition Angel*

**»** Harlan Coben, *Drop Shot*; **»** Michael Connelly, *The Concrete Blonde*; Dick Lochte, *Sleeping Dog*

# EDMUND CRISPIN (1921–78) UK

## THE MOVING TOYSHOP (1946)

*The Moving Toyshop* is set in Oxford. Richard Cadogan is a poet holidaying amid the dreaming spires who wanders idly into a toyshop in the Iffley Road and finds a dead body. No sooner has he made the discovery than he is KO'd by a blow from a blunt instrument. When he comes round, not only has the body disappeared but the toyshop has been mysteriously transformed into a grocery store. Unsurprisingly, no one believes his bizarre story of a vanishing toyshop apart from Gervase Fen, the waspishly witty Professor of English Literature at the university, who sets about proving that the whole, extraordinary saga has its own logic.

Bruce Montgomery was an Oxford friend of Philip Larkin and Kingsley Amis who was known under his own name as a film composer. Writing under the pseudonym of Edmund Crispin, he produced some of the most enjoyable English crime fiction of the 1940s and 1950s and, in Gervase Fen – who unravels complicated crimes with the same zest he applies to the solution of crossword puzzles – he created one of the most memorable and likeable of all academic sleuths. Whether acting as an adviser on a film based, improbably, on the life of Alexander Pope (*Frequent Hearses*), visiting the headmaster of a minor public school at the precise time the school is troubled by murder and mischief (*Love Lies Bleeding*) or standing for parliament in a rural constituency where most of the electors turn out to be memorable and possibly murderous eccentrics (*Buried for Pleasure*), Fen is a splendid creation and the plots in which he figures are perfect blends of macabre humour, offbeat farce and genuinely intriguing mystery. *The Moving Toyshop*, in which the reader shares Richard Cadogan's disorienting sense that the world has been turned upside down, is the best of Crispin's hugely enjoyable books.

### ⮒ Read on

*Love Lies Bleeding*; *The Case of the Gilded Fly*
» Michael Innes, *The Daffodil Affair*; » Gladys Mitchell, *Laurels Are Poison*

---

## READ ON A THEME: OXBRIDGE MURDERS

Gwendoline Butler, *A Coffin for Pandora*
Glyn Daniel, *The Cambridge Murders*
Ruth Dudley Edwards, *Matricide at St Martha's*
Antonia Fraser, *Oxford Blood*
Elizabeth George, *For the Sake of Elena*
Patricia Hall, *Skeleton at the Feast*
» P.D. James, *An Unsuitable Job for a Woman*
» Dorothy L. Sayers, *Gaudy Night*
Jill Paton Walsh, *The Wyndham Case*

# JAMES CRUMLEY (b. 1939) USA

## THE LAST GOOD KISS (1978)

Born in Texas, Crumley served in the army from 1958 to 1961, where his experiences provided the basis for his first novel, *One to Count Cadence*, published in 1969. Unlike many of his contemporaries, Crumley could hardly be described as prolific; he has written only seven novels in a career lasting over thirty years and one interrupted by spells of teaching and scriptwriting in Hollywood, a place he memorably described as 'the Holy Den of Thieves'. Falling under the influence of » Ross Macdonald and, in particular, » Raymond Chandler, Crumley published his first crime novel, *The Wrong Case*, in 1975, following it three years later with *The Last Good Kiss*, which introduced C.W. Sughrue, a likeable, dissolute fellow and, like one or three other American fictional crime investigators, a Vietnam veteran. Crumley alternated appearances by Sughrue and his other 'hero', Milo Milogradovitch, who fought in Korea and who has an eye for the ladies and a nose for cocaine – lots of it – before uniting them in his fifth novel, *Bordersnakes*, in 1997. Apart from his two sybaritic sleuths, Crumley's books share vivid descriptions of their setting: the beautiful wilds of Montana, and keenly observed accounts of male friendships that are usually fomented through bouts of drinking and/or violence.

In *The Last Good Kiss*, which is graced with one of the best opening sentences to appear anywhere, Sughrue is hired to track down an alcoholic writer called Abraham Trahearne by his ex-wife. Trailing him around every watering hole in Montana and all points west, he finds him but, in a classic Crumley move, he also takes on another job, looking for a missing girl, and this leads him, with the drunken Trahearne in tow, to a slew of dark and dangerous degenerates. As the two cases converge, Sughrue's blood is up and violence, inevitably, erupts.

## ☜ Read on

*Bordersnakes*; *Dancing Bear*; *The Final Country*; *The Wrong Case*
» James Lee Burke, *A Stained White Radiance*; Zachary Klein, *Still Among the Living*; » George Pelecanos, *Nick's Trip*; Scott Phillips, *The Ice Harvest*

# COLIN DEXTER (b. 1930) UK

## THE DEAD OF JERICHO (1981)

The partnership between two seemingly mismatched characters, one an investigative genius and the other a plodding but diligent sidekick, has been a mainstay of detective fiction since the days of Holmes and Watson. The alliance Colin Dexter created between the grumpy, opera-loving boozer Chief Inspector Morse and the stolid Detective Sergeant Lewis began in 1975 with the publication of **Last Bus to Woodstock** and has since become the most popular such partnership in contemporary British crime fiction. In **The Dead of Jericho** (the title refers to a curiously named area of Oxford, the city where the two policemen work), Morse meets a woman, Anne Scott, at a party and is attracted to her. When he visits her in Jericho, she seems not to be at home. He later discovers that she was there but that she was dead. A verdict of suicide fails to convince him that all of the truth about Anne Scott's death has emerged and he determines to investigate further. Fuelled by his usual combination of beer and misanthropy, Morse is this time also haunted by the guilty feeling that he might somehow have prevented her death. With the faithful Lewis in tow, he sets about proving that there was much more to Anne Scott's death than was thought.

Those who only know Morse from TV might well be surprised by the books, particularly those which, like *The Dead of Jericho*, were published before he became a star of the screen. He is a younger, even more prickly version of the character John Thaw played in the TV series and the relationship between him and Lewis is different. What readers coming to the books from the TV series will recognize and appreciate is the complexity of the character Dexter created and the clever use he made of the Oxford settings to produce some of the finest British crime fiction of the past thirty years.

## ⮑ Read on

*Last Bus to Woodstock*; *The Way Through the Woods*
» Reginald Hill, *An Advancement of Learning*; Peter Lovesey, *The Last Detective*; » Peter Robinson, *The Hanging Valley*; Andrew Taylor, *Call the Dying*

## READ ON A THEME: POLICE PROCEDURALS (BRITISH)

Clare Curzon, *A Meeting of Minds*
Alex Gray, *Never Somewhere Else*
John Harvey, *Still Water*
Graham Hurley, *Cut to Black*
Bill James, *The Lolita Man*
Quintin Jardine, *Dead and Buried*
David Lawrence, *The Dead Sit Round in a Ring*
Stuart Pawson, *Last Reminder*
Sheila Radley, *Death and the Maiden*
R.D. Wingfield, *Hard Frost*

# MICHAEL DIBDIN (b. 1947) UK

## DEAD LAGOON (1994)

Michael Dibdin's creation, Aurelio Zen, investigator for the Criminalpol section of the Italian Ministry of the Interior, is one of the most interesting protagonists in contemporary crime fiction, a rounded and convincing character who struggles to retain what integrity he can amid the corruption of the society in which he works. Grimly realistic and clear-sighted about the labyrinthine bureaucracy that surrounds him, he knows that, where power and money are involved, his investigations are unlikely to flourish and yet he continues to believe that the truth is worth a struggle. Not above bending the rules himself, he still cares about reaching as much of the truth as he can and the novels entertainingly follow his devious route towards that goal.

In *Dead Lagoon*, the best of the series so far, Zen returns to his native city of Venice and finds that he is no longer at home there. Ostensibly, he is looking into the bizarre persecution of a half-mad old contessa but his real, private mission, subsidized by a rich family, is to investigate the disappearance of an American millionaire from his island-home in the lagoon. The Venice Zen finds is not the city of tourist guides and Canaletto vistas but one where decay and corruption hold sway and the population festers with resentment towards the tourism which supports the economy. Friends from childhood have become strangers. Many of them have become supporters of the ruthless and unscrupulous leader of a separatist party intent on the impossible dream of returning Venice to its old position as an independent city-state and they plan to use Zen for their own purposes. As he struggles with chicanery and double-dealing, with unhappy memories and ambiguous revelations about his family history, he realizes that he is as out of place in his native city as the tourists who surround him.

## ⮯ Read on

*Cabal*; *Medusa*; *Dirty Tricks* (one of the best of Dibdin's non-Zen novels); *The Last Sherlock Holmes Story* (an ingenious pastiche)
Andrea Camilleri, *The Shape of Water*; » Donna Leon, *Fatal Remedies*; Carlo Lucarelli, *Almost Blue*

# SIR ARTHUR CONAN DOYLE (1859–1930) UK

## THE SIGN OF FOUR (1890)

*The Sign of Four* finds Sherlock Holmes and Dr Watson in their rooms in Baker Street, the city around them swathed in a dense yellow fog, and the great detective administering to himself a seven per cent solution of cocaine in order to alleviate his boredom and depression. A knock at the door heralds the arrival of Miss Mary Morstan, a beautiful and distressed young woman with a strange tale. Following the mysterious disappearance of her father, she has received every year since the gift of a large and lustrous pearl. After six years, she has been summoned to meet the unknown donor and enlists the aid of Holmes and Watson. As he probes this strange affair, Holmes solves the mystery of Miss Morstan's missing father, uncovers a hoard of Indian treasure, crosses swords with a one-legged rogue and his devilish companion, and enlists the services of a helpful hound, of non-Baskerville variety. A miniature masterpiece of suspense and deduction, the novella concludes with Watson finding true love, while his friend, spurning such distractions, once again accedes to the colder, more insidious charms of the white powder.

The most famous of the longer Holmes stories is undoubtedly *The Hound of the Baskervilles*, in which the detective comes face to face with a gigantic and seemingly supernatural dog on the moors of Devon, but *The Sign of Four* is, in many ways, an even more archetypal Sherlockian adventure. The great sleuth and his sidekick are forever associated with the fog-enshrouded streets of late Victorian London and no story better embodies the association than this narrative of greed, fear and a long-delayed revenge. Reaching a crescendo with a breathless chase down the Thames, *The Sign of Four* shows Holmes at the peak of his deductive powers, unveiling the truth behind events that seem inexplicable to lesser mortals.

### ⮒ Read on

*The Hound of the Baskervilles*; *A Study in Scarlet*, *The Valley of Fear* August Derleth, *The Adventures of Solar Pons*; **»** Fergus Hume, *The Mystery of a Hansom Cab*; Nicholas Meyer, *The Seven Per Cent Solution*

## THE MEMOIRS OF SHERLOCK HOLMES

Although longer narratives like *The Hound of the Baskervilles* and *The Sign of Four* are justly admired, most Sherlock Holmes aficionados would agree that their hero is seen to his best advantage in the short stories. First published in *The Strand* magazine, and then collected in five volumes, the stories show the supremely rational detective, accompanied by his dependable sidekick Dr Watson, in single-minded pursuit of the truth behind a succession of seemingly insoluble mysteries. The first collection, *The Adventures of Sherlock Holmes*, includes many fine tales, including such well-known ones as 'The Red-Headed League' and 'The Adventure of the Speckled Band', but the best of all the volumes is *The Memoirs of Sherlock Holmes*, eleven stories in which the detective's eccentric genius is brilliantly and variously displayed. 'The Gloria Scott' and 'The Musgrave Ritual' both have a younger Holmes, in the days before he met Watson, showing early signs of the startling deductive powers which were to make him famous. In 'Silver Blaze', a trip out of London to Dartmoor (later scene of his encounter with the hellish Baskerville hound) finds him investigating the bizarre disappearance of a champion racehorse and the apparent murder of its trainer. 'The Greek Interpreter' introduces Watson, and readers, to Holmes's even smarter brother Mycroft. The volume reaches its conclusion with 'The Final Problem', the story in which Doyle famously tried to rid himself of his own creation by pitting Holmes against the 'Napoleon of Crime', Professor Moriarty, and apparently sending them both plummeting to their deaths over the Reichenbach Falls. As everyone knows, Holmes fans refused to accept his death and Doyle was later obliged to restore him to life and involve him in further adventures but the great detective was never quite the same after Reichenbach. There were occasional great stories still to come but none of the later collections matched the quality to be found on every page of *The Memoirs of Sherlock Holmes*.

## ≋ Read on

*The Adventures of Sherlock Holmes*; *The Return of Sherlock Holmes*
**»** G.K. Chesterton, *The Innocence of Father Brown*; Jacques Futrelle, *The Thinking Machine*; Arthur Morrison, *Martin Hewitt, Investigator*

## READ ON A THEME: HOLMES BEYOND DOYLE

Caleb Carr, *The Italian Secretary*
Mitch Cullin, *A Slight Trick of the Mind*
» Michael Dibdin, *The Last Sherlock Holmes Story*
Adrian Conan Doyle and » John Dickson Carr, *The Exploits of Sherlock Holmes*
» Loren D. Estleman, *Dr Jekyll and Mr Holmes*
Laurie King, *The Bee-Keeper's Apprentice*
Larry Millett, *The Disappearance of Sherlock Holmes*
Jamyang Norbu, *The Mandala of Sherlock Holmes*

# JAMES ELLROY (b. 1948) USA

## THE BLACK DAHLIA (1987)

A figure who could have easily lurched from the pages of one of his own crime novels, James Ellroy was born in Los Angeles to parents on the fringes of show business who divorced when he was eight. When he was ten, Ellroy's mother was strangled and her body dumped in an ivy patch by a killer who was never found. Already a keen fan of crime magazines and books, on his eleventh birthday, Ellroy read about LA's most notorious unsolved murder: the 1947 Black Dahlia killing, in which Elizabeth Short was tortured and killed, her naked body hacked in two.

According to his memoir, *My Dark Places*, Ellroy 'read the Dahlia story a hundred times'. A photo of Short revealed a pretty woman with 'hair swept up and back – like a 1940s portrait shot of my mother'. As he succinctly put it, 'It sent me way off the deep end'.

After a troubled adolescence and young adulthood, Ellroy cleaned up his act and started writing visceral and surreally violent crime novels, including a trilogy about LAPD cop Lloyd Hopkins. His seventh book, *The Black Dahlia,* appeared in 1987 and was a vast leap forward in every way. The first of four volumes subsequently dubbed *The LA Quartet*, it is an unbelievably powerful novel and one that finally pays tribute to the two women who had continued to haunt him – his mother and Elizabeth Short. Using the Dahlia case as the backdrop for a story of two LA cops, Bucky Bleichert and Lee Blanchard, who become friends and partners, Ellroy meticulously constructs an epic and hugely ambitious portrayal of police corruption, a twisted love triangle and myriad layers of deceit, duplicity and desire, all set in a brilliantly depicted LA: a city seething with fear, paranoia and all manner of tawdry passions.

## ⮂ Read on

*The Big Nowhere*; *LA Confidential*; *White Jazz* (the other novels in the LA Quartet); *American Tabloid*

Jack Bludis, *The Big Switch*; Robert Campbell, *In La-La Land We Trust*; » Michael Connelly, *The Last Coyote*; » James Crumley, *Bordersnakes*

# LOREN D. ESTLEMAN (b. 1952) USA

## DOWNRIVER (1988)

A writer whose career has spanned just over a quarter of a century and has taken in several genres, including Westerns and historical fiction, Loren D. Estleman is probably best known for his crime novels, most of which have featured private eye Amos Walker. If this amiable, world-weary investigator is the star of the show, then worthy of equal billing is the city of Detroit, the setting for all his adventures. Memorably described by Estleman, with a mixture of affection, cynicism and disenchantment, as 'the place where the American dream stalled and sat rusting in the rain', the Motor City is Walker's beat and he prowls its crumbling, oil-slicked streets as ably as Philip Marlowe patrolled the sunlit hills and boulevards of Raymond Chandler's Los Angeles.

In *Downriver*, Walker is hired by Richard DeVries, a black man just released from prison, having served twenty years for arson and robbing an armoured car during the riots of 1967. He claims that he was framed for a murder that was committed during the robbery and that he is now due the $200,000 that was never found after the heist, convincing Walker that he has earned his right to the money: 'I paid for it and now it's mine.' One of the men DeVries wants was a so-called revolutionary and the one who urged him to throw the firebomb during the riot, but who has since become a hotshot automobile executive, with a glamorous ex-wife and a lot of reasons for wanting to keep hidden the violent events of two decades ago. Before long, Walker is up to his neck in trouble as he starts to uncover some very nasty secrets. Witty, exciting and laced with fast-paced action and some of the crispest dialogue around, *Downriver* is Estleman at his best, which is pretty damn good.

### 📖 Read on

*The Glass Highway*; *Motor City Blue*; *A Smile on the Face of the Tiger* (all Amos Walker novels); *Whiskey River* (the first of a series of novels in which Estleman explores the criminal history of Detroit is set in 1928) » Elmore Leonard, *City Primeval*; » Robert B. Parker, *The Widening Gyre*

# ROBERT FERRIGNO (b. 1947) USA

### FLINCH (2001)

Former journalist Ferrigno has written nine highly entertaining novels, set mainly in the sun-kissed idyll and moral vacuum of southern California, adding his unique perspective to that well-explored terrain. Often eschewing the usual police officer or private detective, Ferrigno instead peoples his novels with Californian types – journalists, plastic surgeons, rock stars, lawyers, body-builders and the occasional scientist, as well as sundry individuals stylishly subsisting on the fringes of the film industry. Heading this colourful, often garish cast is the typical Ferrigno anti-hero: a charming, shrewd maverick with an idiosyncratic, but acute sense of justice, always ready to fight for what he feels is right and, in the process, successfully winning the admiration, and more, of a beautiful woman. *Flinch* finds resourceful reporter Jimmy Gage returning from Europe to California and becoming embroiled in the hunt for a vicious serial killer. As well as continuing a perennial duel with his brother Jonathan, a successful plastic surgeon who has recently married his sibling's former lover, Jimmy is also coping with his increasing attraction to police detective Jane Holt, who is not only investigating the killings but looking into Jimmy's life as well. Slick, sexy and tautly written, this may well be Ferrigno's finest offering.

Many of Ferrigno's books are separate adventures, although the same characters feature in *The Cheshire Moon* and *Dead Man's Dance*, as well as *Flinch* and *Scavenger Hunt*, with both of these protagonists being journalists. *Heartbreaker* starts off in Ferrigno's home turf of Florida before swiftly moving to LA, and features an ex-undercover cop battling a psychotic smuggler, while *The Wake-Up* covers the exploits of a former government agent as he confronts art forgers and drug dealers. His latest novel, *Prayers for the Assassin*, is a bold departure in that it's set in the very near future and has a more political edge.

### ⮂ Read on
*The Cheshire Moon*; *Dead Man's Dance*; *Dead Silent*; *Heartbreaker*
» Harlan Coben, *Fade Away*; Arthur Lyons, *Three With a Bullet*

# G.M. FORD (b. 1945) USA

## WHO IN HELL IS WANDA FUCA? (1995)
There have been plenty of attempts in the last twenty years to bring the old-style private eye of the » Hammett and » Chandler era into the modern world but few have been as engaging and entertaining as G.M. Ford's shot at it in his novels featuring the Seattle-based investigator Leo

Waterman. Half wisecracking smartass and half unreconstructed hippy still in thrall to the ideals of the sixties, Waterman ambles through a series of unlikely and often very funny adventures in his native city. Aided, and occasionally impeded, by his sidekicks, a gang of 'residentially-challenged devotees of cheap alcohol' (i.e. drunken bums), he succeeds, despite the odds, in triumphing over the bad guys. Waterman made his first appearance in *Who in Hell is Wanda Fuca?*, a book which Ford claimed, as others have done before him, that he wrote after reading a particularly poor crime novel and deciding that he could do better. Given the job of tracking down the runaway granddaughter of a local bigshot, Leo stumbles into a plot that involves polluters dumping toxic waste illegally and environmental activists prepared to go to almost any lengths to stop them. Both sides seem equally unenthusiastic about his enquiries and he and his dysfunctional bunch of boozers have to sharpen what wits they have as they look to unearth the truth.

Sadly, Leo Waterman's career seems to have come to an end. The sixth book, *The Deader the Better*, appeared in 2000 and there are no signs of more to come. His creator's career, however, has continued apace and Ford has published several books in a new series featuring a true crime writer named Frank Corso. They are excellent examples of a darker brand of crime fiction but fans of Leo Waterman will none the less mourn the departure of one of the most memorable PIs of recent decades.

## 🦢 Read on

*The Bum's Rush*; *Slow Burn*; *Fury* (the first and the best of Ford's Frank Corso books)

» John D. MacDonald, *A Deadly Shade of Gold*

# DICK FRANCIS (b. 1920) UK

## DEAD CERT (1962)

Authenticity is a priceless commodity in crime fiction and former champion jockey Dick Francis offered it in spades when he published his first novel, *Dead Cert*, in 1962. The book set the pattern for the novels which Francis continued to publish for the next forty years. Alan York is a Rhodesian-born amateur jockey riding in England. During a race at Maidenstone, he is several lengths behind the favourite, ridden by his close friend Major Bill Davidson, when the horse falls at a fence, killing Davidson. York is the only one who sees that the fatal accident was no accident at all but was caused by wire stretched across the fence. When he returns to the scene, the wire has been removed. The authorities are unconvinced that foul play was involved and York is obliged to investigate Davidson's death himself. Within days, he is attacked and threatened with dire consequences if he pursues his enquiries. It becomes clear that he has stumbled across a wide-ranging racing scam. Another jockey, who has been taking bribes in return for deliberately holding horses back in important races, is found murdered; a gang of taxi-drivers turned mobsters is terrorizing small businesses in Brighton with demands for protection money; another supposed accident lands York in hospital. When he recovers, he can rely only on his own courage and resourcefulness in the increasingly desperate struggle to trap the mastermind behind all the chicanery and violence.

Francis has his faults as a writer. His characterization, particularly of women, is a bit perfunctory and his plots are often creaky. What he does offer in all his novels are a real insider's view of the racing business and a genuine ability to ratchet up the tension as amateur heroes like Alan

York slowly edge towards the truth about the crimes and conspiracies into which they have been plunged.

### ⮒ Read on
*Bonecrack*; *Comeback*; *Forfeit*; *For Kicks*
Stephen Dobyns, *Saratoga Headhunter*; John Francome, *Inside Track*;
Sam Llewellyn, *Deadeye*

# ERLE STANLEY GARDNER (1889–1970) USA

## THE CASE OF THE TERRIFIED TYPIST (1956)
Perry Mason, the master of courtroom drama created by Erle Stanley Gardner in the 1930s, is one of the most popular of all characters in crime fiction. Sales of the Perry Mason books, of which there are dozens and dozens, can be counted in the millions and the well-known and the affectionately remembered TV series of the 1950s and 1960s, in which Mason was played by Raymond Burr, only added to the character's success. In some ways, singling out one of the books is a pointless task. Quite deliberately, they follow a formula. In many of them, a client in trouble, often accused of murder, approaches Perry Mason. The case against him or her seems open and shut. Conviction looks inevitable but, in a courtroom confrontation that provides the climax to the book, Mason brilliantly outsmarts his adversaries, often by introducing some new and revelatory piece of evidence at the last minute.

*The Case of the Terrified Typist* is one of the most enjoyable and typical titles in the series. A temporary typist arrives at Perry Mason's office to work on an important legal brief. During her break, she disappears and becomes the chief suspect in a burglary in the office building. As the plot unfolds and a possible murder is added to the list of crimes (the assumed victim, whose body has not been found, may just have absconded), Mason needs urgently to track down the missing typist. Series characters Della Street, Mason's secretary, and private eye Paul Drake both have their roles to play in a narrative that twists and turns towards a satisfyingly surprising ending. Erle Stanley Gardner began his career in the heyday of the pulp magazines (he was a contributor to the legendary *Black Mask* in the 1920s and 1930s) and his books always carry echoes of that era but Perry Mason was at his best in the novels published in the 1950s, of which *The Case of the Terrified Typist* is one of the finest.

### ⮑ Read on

*The Case of the Glamorous Ghost*; *The Case of the Hesitant Hostess*; *The Case of the Howling Dog*; *The Case of the Sulky Girl* (the first Perry Mason)

# MICHAEL GILBERT (1912–2006) UK

## SMALLBONE DECEASED (1950)

Horniman, Birley and Crane is one of the most respectable and respected firms of solicitors in London, so the discovery of the body of one of its trustees in a large deed box is an unexpected and inexplicable breach in the natural order of things. All the members of the firm's staff, with the sole exception of the newly arrived Henry Bohun, are under suspicion. The intelligent and resourceful Bohun is recruited by Inspector Hazelrigg (a recurring character in Gilbert's novels) to provide an insider's assistance with the investigation. Bohun, who suffers from a rare form of insomnia which means that he is alert for far more hours out of the twenty-four than the rest of us, soon finds that most of his colleagues have secrets to hide. Two of them are conducting a clandestine love affair. Another is moonlighting with a rival solicitors, snatching clients away from Horniman, Birley and Crane. The firm itself has long been in financial trouble and the retirement prospects for the partners are less than rosy. There are motives in plenty for the murder. Gilbert gleefully scatters red herrings throughout his puzzling plot, a second murder adds urgency to Bohun and Hazelrigg's investigation and the mystery is skilfully maintained until the final, unexpected denouement.

Michael Gilbert was himself a lawyer so he knew the world of which he wrote in *Smallbone Deceased*. Over the decades from the 1940s to the 1990s, he published crime novels in a variety of forms, from well-crafted police procedurals featuring Inspector Petrella, to spy thrillers involving the counter-intelligence agents Calder and Behrens, but it is his legal mysteries which have proved most lasting in their charm and sophisticated storytelling. Of these, *Smallbone Deceased*, with its elaborately worked out plot and engaging hero, literally unsleeping in the pursuit of truth, is the best.

## ⮑ Read on

*Close Quarters*; *Fear to Travel*

Sarah Caudwell, *Thus Was Adonis Murdered*; **»** Cyril Hare, *Tragedy at Law*; **»** P.D. James, *A Certain Justice*; John Mortimer, *Rumpole of the Bailey*

# DAVID GOODIS (1917–67) USA

## DARK PASSAGE (1946)

After graduating with a degree in journalism in 1937, Goodis spent a year writing advertising copy and his first novel, the Hemingway-influenced *Retreat From Oblivion*, a tale of infidelity that has itself retreated into oblivion. Moving to New York, he wrote for pulp magazines, pounding out horror, western and mystery yarns at a cent a word, and also writing radio serials, including episodes for *House of Mystery* and *Superman*. In 1946, he wrote *Dark Passage*, which was serialized in the respectable and prestigious *Saturday Evening Post* and sold to Warner Brothers, who filmed it starring Humphrey Bogart and Lauren Bacall. The following year, he wrote two more books: the novella, *Nightfall*, filmed by Jacques Tourneur, and *Behold This Woman*, a lurid, masochistic work. Following six years scriptwriting in Hollywood, a period and place that he disliked, Goodis continued producing novels, successfully tapping into the burgeoning post-war paperback market. The first of these, *Cassidy's Girl*, published in 1951, sold over a million copies, and was followed by a dozen others, all depicting losers cursed by fate and destined to fail. Many were filmed, with varying results, but none of the screen versions had the bleakness and dark power of the originals and when Goodis died in 1967, few were in print.

*Dark Passage* was published in hardback only after it had been filmed and is the grim story of Vincent Parry, a man falsely accused of murdering a wife whom he did not love, his protests of innocence netting him a life sentence in San Quentin. Breaking out, his face changed forever by a quack surgeon, Parry hooks up with a mysterious young woman as he struggles to discover who framed him for his wife's murder. Once outside, however, he finds that he has just gone from one prison to another, and this time, there is no escape.

🎬 **Film version:** *Dark Passage* (1946)

📖 **Read on**
*Down There*; *The Moon in the Gutter*; *Nightfall*
Horace McCoy, *Kiss Tomorrow Goodbye*; » Jim Thompson, *The Nothing Man*; » Cornell Woolrich, *The Bride Wore Black*

# JOE GORES (b. 1931) USA

## GONE, NO FORWARDING (1978)
Gores started writing in the 1950s and, alongside » Dashiell Hammett, he is one of the few crime authors who have based their fiction on personal experience. While Hammett spent several happy years working for the Pinkerton Detective Agency in San Francisco, Gores was

a private eye and repo man for twelve years, fondly saying of this period: 'I loved detective work, I truly loved it.' His exploits formed the basis of the novels and stories in his superb DKA series, concerning a San Francisco-based agency called Daniel Kearny Associates, and which consists primarily of Kearny himself, his old colleague Patrick Michael O'Bannon, Larry Ballard, Bart Heslip and Gisèle Marc. Alongside this wide range of personalities (O'Bannon is Irish and, like Kearny, middle-aged; Ballard is young, white and idealistic and best friends with Heslip, who is young, black, hip but not ambitious, while Marc is very ambitious, young and smart), the books are all laced with a deadpan humour, are highly detailed and full of suspense.

Gores has also written several other novels, including *Hammett*, filmed by Francis Ford Coppola and Wim Wenders and co-scripted by Ross Thomas, *Interface*, *Wolf Time* and *Dead Man*. He has also written over fifty stories, many about DKA, and penned scripts for such television shows as *Columbo*, *Magnum PI* and *Kojak*. The DKA books represent his best work, however, and have so far numbered one collection of stories and six novels, of which *Gone, No Forwarding* is the third. Hunting down a prostitute who is on the run, Kearny and his agents are in danger of losing their licence and find that they have been set up by some major-league heavies, including a Mob-connected lawyer. As they race across country and against time, their frantic search leads then towards danger and death.

## ⮂ Read on

*Dead Skip*; *Final Notice*; *32 Cadillacs* (all DKA novels); *Hammett*
» Dashiell Hammett, *The Maltese Falcon*

# SUE GRAFTON (b. 1940) USA

## A IS FOR ALIBI (1986)

Who knows what Sue Grafton will do when she writes her twenty-seventh book, but so far she is been doing a great job of making the alphabet a lot more exciting and interesting. Alongside » Sara Paretsky and Marcia Muller, she was in the vanguard of a troop of female crime writers in the 1980s and so far she has lasted the course extremely well, as has her heroine, feisty and resourceful private investigator Kinsey Millhone. Born in Santa Teresa, California (a fictional version of Santa Barbara borrowed from Ross Macdonald), and orphaned when she was five, Kinsey joined the local police department, but left after two years, due to their attitude towards women and bureaucratic constraints. After two brief and unsuccessful marriages, she became a private investigator, going freelance after a couple of years. On its alphabetical progression, the series has consistently developed and Kinsey has also evolved. As her cases become darker and more violent, she is shaped by her increasingly sinister experiences, and so her personality grows more complex and intriguing.

In *A is for Alibi* she is investigating the murder of Laurence Fife, a successful, ruthless divorce attorney and ladies' man, who was killed eight years ago. The woman hiring her is the dead man's widow, who has just been paroled after spending those eight years inside for supposedly killing the man she loved. Now she wants Kinsey to find the real killer and the intrepid sleuth has to strip away the lies of the past and uncover some very nasty secrets in her bid to learn the truth. Rearing their ugly heads along the way are adultery, deceit and murder, including another eight-year-old killing and also one that is much more recent. Sharp and smart, tender as well as tough, Kinsey is a totally convincing and compelling character and, as for the series featuring her, there really is no better place to start than here.

## 🍃 Read on

*E is for Evidence*, *I is for Innocent* and *O is for Outlaw* are among the best alphabetical excursions of Kinsey Milhone so far

Linda Barnes, *Deep Pockets*; Marcia Muller, *The Shape of Dread*; » Sara Paretsky, *Indemnity Only*

---

### READ ON A THEME: FEMALE PRIVATE EYES

Linda Barnes, *Cold Case* (Carlotta Carlyle)
Liza Cody, *Dupe* (Anna Lee)
Janet Dawson, *Where the Bodies Are Buried* (Jeri Howard)
Sarah Dunant, *Birthmarks* (Hannah Wolfe)
Janet Evanovich, *One for the Money* (Stephanie Plum)
Karen Kijewski, *Katwalk* (Kat Colorado)
Laura Lippman, *Baltimore Blues* (Tess Monaghan)
Val McDermid, *Common Murder* (Lindsay Gordon)
» Sara Paretsky, *Bitter Medicine* (V.I. Warshawski)
Sandra Scoppettone, *Everything You Have is Mine* (Lauren Laurano)

---

# JAMES W. HALL (b. 1947) USA

## UNDER COVER OF DAYLIGHT (1987)

One of the many writers who have succumbed to Florida's balmy, torrid charms and found it to be the perfect setting for crime fiction, Hall is one of the best of the current practitioners, with thirteen novels to his credit, as well as a book of stories, an essay collection and four volumes of verse. The novels are all, at least partly, set in the sunshine state and eight of them have featured as their protagonist a man just called Thorn, who was introduced in Hall's debut, *Under Cover of Daylight*. A highly intriguing individual, Thorn is a classic anti-hero, an amiable figure but also moody and introspective, who is just this side of being a sociopath and who, despite his many adventures, remains, in the words of his creator, 'simply so reluctant to get involved in the affairs of the world'. One of the best of the non-Thorn novels is *Body Language*, published in 1998, which features beautiful police photographer Alexandra Rafferty. She teams up with Thorn in 2003's *Blackwater Sound*, when reluctantly he has to confront the unsettling and unstable Braswell family, a once-powerful clan riven by dark secrets and desperate to claw back their former wealth and prestige.

*Under Cover of Daylight* is disturbing and extremely compelling, calmly opening with Thorn, a nineteen-year-old orphan, killing the drunk driver who had run down his parents fifteen years earlier. Flashing forward twenty years, he now leads a solitary, seemingly quiet life in the Florida Keys, but inwardly still struggles to come to terms with his guilty act of revenge. But when his adoptive mother is raped and murdered, and Thorn hunts for her attacker, his violent past returns in the form of a beautiful and mysterious woman, forcing him to realize that killing and vengeance have no limits.

### ⋐ Read on

*Blackwater Sound*; *Bones of Coral*; *Mean High Tide*; *Squall Line* (all Thorn novels); *Body Language*

Tim Dorsey, *Florida Roadkill*; » G.M. Ford, *A Blind Eye*; » John D. MacDonald, *The Dreadful Lemon Sky*

# DASHIELL HAMMETT (1894–1961) USA

## THE GLASS KEY (1931)

By the time *The Glass Key*, Hammett's fourth, and penultimate, novel was published, he had virtually peaked as a crime novelist, having produced *Red Harvest*, *The Dain Curse* and, perhaps the finest of all private eye novels, *The Maltese Falcon*, in a blazing two-year period. It might have seemed that many more novels were to come but all that was left for this talented and original writer was the slight, if hugely popular *The Thin Man*, a handful of stories, enormously well paid, but unrewarding film work and a twenty-year slow fade of drinking, spending vast sums of money, chasing women and dodging deadlines.

Before this, though, he produced what was probably his finest work, *The Glass Key*, a beautifully written and mesmerizing story of political corruption, friendship, loyalty and love of the triangular kind. Set in an anonymous American city near New York, it tells the story of a politician who is in love with the daughter of a senator, whom he is helping to get re-elected. Also interested in her is his friend and lieutenant, the cool and charismatic Ned Beaumont, the novel's protagonist and a beguiling character. A gambler and fixer, the laconic Beaumont is smart and fearless, and much given to smoothing his moustache when hatching a plan. As in the best of Hammett's work, the action comes thick and fast, so that murder, the deadly machinations of a rival gang boss, duplicity and double-dealing all flash through the pages, scenes zipping by like shots from a gun. Hammett proved himself to be a master of American vernacular and was capable, for a tantalizingly brief period, to dash off page after breathless page of razor-sharp, streamlined action, along with prose that was intelligent, warm and witty, and he excelled himself here. He could never top it and he barely bothered even trying to, but this masterpiece was surely enough.

**Film versions:** *The Glass Key* (1935); *The Glass Key* (1942)

## Read on
*The Dain Curse*; *The Maltese Falcon*; *Red Harvest*; *The Thin Man*
» Joe Gores, *Hammett*; Peter Rabe, *Dig My Grave Deep*; Raoul Whitfield, *Green Ice*

# JOSEPH HANSEN (1923–2004) USA

## FADEOUT (1970)

Although born in South Dakota, Hansen moved in 1936, to southern California, where he lived for the rest of his life. Although he married in 1943 and fathered a daughter, Hansen was a homosexual, and his early fiction was written under the pseudonym of James Colton and published by small presses specializing in erotica. *Strange Marriage*, published in 1965, is considered to be a particularly good example of contemporary gay pulp fiction. To some extent, it is probably autobiographical, since it deals with a West Coast couple whose married life is an unorthodox but successful compromise (Hansen's wife, Jane Bancroft, was a lesbian). Hansen wrote gay mainstream fiction in the 1980s and '90s, two 1970s' novels under the pseudonym Rose Brocks, a volume of poetry, and much short fiction, but his greatest achievement was the Dave Brandstetter series. Begun in 1970 and written over a twenty-year period, this consists of a dozen crime novels featuring insurance investigator Brandstetter, a sceptical, extremely thorough man who is also gay. His sexuality aside, he differs from most other fictional sleuths of the period in that he is not a private eye hired by an individual client and does not get involved with crimes like theft, blackmail or kidnapping. Instead, he works for an insurance company and investigates suspicious deaths, usually murders, and by solving the case, saves his company money.

A fine debut, *Fadeout* finds Brandstetter looking into the apparent death of a singer, Fox Olson, whose car has plunged off a storm-swept bridge. A claim is filed, but no body has been found, leading

Brandstetter to wonder whether the victim is actually dead. Persistent enquiries among family, fans, friends and enemies only add to his suspicions, but he has still to find Olson before someone else does, or else this time his death might just be real.

### ⮑ Read on

*A Country of Old Men*; *The Little Dog Laughed*; *Skinflick*
George Baxt, *A Queer Kind of Death*; Edgar Box (Gore Vidal), *Three by Box*; Greg Herren, *Bourbon Street Blues*; Greg Lilly, *Fingering the Family Jewels*

---

## READ ON A THEME: GAY AND LESBIAN DETECTIVES

George Baxt, *A Queer Kind of Love* (Pharaoh Love)
Anthony Bidulka, *Amuse Bouche* (Russell Quant)
Michael Craft, *Body Language* (Mark Manning)
Sarah Dreher, *Bad Company* (Stoner McTavish)
Stella Duffy, *Beneath the Blonde* (Saz Martin)
Katherine V. Forrest, *Murder by Tradition* (Kate Delafield)
Josh Lanyon, *The Hell You Say* (Adrien English)
Val McDermid, *Report for Murder* (Lindsay Gordon)
Michael Nava, *The Burning Plain* (Henry Rios)
Barbara Wilson, *Gaudi Afternoon* (Cassandra Reilly)
Mary Wings, *She Came Too Late* (Emma Victor)

---

# CYRIL HARE (1900–58) UK

## WHEN THE WIND BLOWS (1949)

Under the pseudonym of Cyril Hare, the county court judge Alfred Gordon Clark wrote a number of classic detective stories which are characterized by a dry wit and an insider's knowledge of the often bizarre workings of the English legal system. His two recurring characters are Inspector Mallett, a Scotland Yard detective who first appeared in Hare's debut novel *Tenant for Death* in 1937, and the unassuming, gentlemanly barrister Francis Pettigrew, who plays a significant role in *Tragedy at Law*, Hare's own favourite among his books. *Tragedy at Law* is indeed a fine and witty novel and Hare provides in it a subtly rounded portrait of the likeable, slightly melancholy Pettigrew but, seen simply as a crime novel, it is arguably less effective than some of Hare's other books. In *When the Wind Blows*, for example, Pettigrew is married and living in a small town in the imaginary southern county of Markshire where he and his wife are leading lights in the local orchestra. The novel's plot is set in motion when the orchestra's performance of Mozart's Prague Symphony is rudely interrupted by the murder of its first violinist. Pettigrew proves a reluctant detective. The energetic, slightly dim Inspector Trimble is on the case and the retiring barrister has no wish to interfere but his help and his legal expertise eventually turn out to be essential to unmasking the guilty man. Hare provides both motive and opportunity for the murderer with great ingenuity, he puts his knowledge of the law to good use, as always, and the background of music-making in a small provincial town, with all its small rivalries and rows, is sharply but affectionately sketched. Before his death, at the relatively early age of 57, Cyril Hare went on to write other Pettigrew novels and to create another offbeat central character, the learned Czech academic Dr Bottwink, in *An English Murder*. But *When the Wind Blows* remains the best introduction to a crime novelist whose work deserves a wider following.

### ≋ Read on

*Tragedy at Law*; *An English Murder*
Henry Cecil, *No Bail for the Judge*; **»** Michael Gilbert, *Smallbone Deceased*

# THOMAS HARRIS (b. 1940) USA

## RED DRAGON (1981)

A writer whose extraordinary popularity is based entirely on three novels and their subsequent cinematic adaptations, Thomas Harris is also something of a rarity in that this success has been due to a villain rather than a hero, and the bedside manners of his serial killer, Dr Hannibal Lecter, have kept millions of readers up at night. After his 1973 thriller, *Black Sunday*, former newspaper reporter and editor Harris published *Red Dragon* in 1981, which featured the first appearance by Lecter, a highly capable psychiatrist and monstrous sociopath and one of modern fiction's most chilling and memorable characters. The book was filmed as *Manhunter*, but it was in Lecter's second appearance, in the 1988 breakthrough novel, *The Silence of the Lambs*, and the 1990 film version, that the bad doctor exploded on to popular consciousness.

In *Red Dragon*, much of the action involving Lecter takes place off stage, with the cannibalistic doctor being described by Will Graham, the FBI agent who caught him. Graham is a highly skilled operative who has the ability to tune in to the way serial killers think, and who still bears the scars, mental as well as physical, of his tussle with Lecter. In retirement, Graham is asked by his former boss, FBI chief Jack Crawford, to help the Bureau track down a killer dubbed 'The Tooth Fairy', a man who has already slaughtered two families. To psych himself up, Graham visits Lecter in prison, but has to tread carefully since the doctor can insinuate himself into a person's mind, especially someone like Graham, already haunted by the possibility that there may be a perilously fine line between himself and the killers he hunts. Unbelievably tense and exciting, and fascinating in its portrayal of FBI procedures, this is one of the finest crime novels of the last fifty years.

◣ **Film versions:** *Manhunter* (1986); *Red Dragon* (2002)

≋ **Read on**
*The Silence of the Lambs*; *Hannibal*
Philip Kerr, *A Philosophical Investigation*; Joseph Koenig, *Floater*;
James Patterson, *Kiss the Girls*

## READONATHEME: SERIAL KILLERS

David Baldacci, *Hour Game*
Mark Billingham, *Sleepyhead*
Caleb Carr, *The Alienist*
Jeffery Deaver, *The Coffin Dancer*
Tess Gerritsen, *The Surgeon*
Mo Hayder, *Birdman*
John Katzenbach, *The Analyst*
Faye Kellerman, *Straight Into Darkness*
Jack Kerley, *The Hundredth Man*
Val McDermid, *The Mermaids Singing*
Ridley Pearson, *The Angel Maker*
John Sandford, *Rules of Prey*

# CARL HIAASEN (b. 1953) USA

## TOURIST SEASON (1986)

After writing several novels in collaboration, Hiaasen made his first appearance as a solo author with **Tourist Season** and its plot sets the pattern for much of his later fiction. A band of anti-tourist terrorists is on the loose in Florida, led by a rogue newspaperman appalled by the destruction of the state's natural beauty and resources. The head of Miami's Chamber of Commerce has been found dead with a toy rubber alligator lodged in his throat. More murders follow. Another reporter turned private eye is given the job of tracking down the terrorists, a task which soon turns into an excursion along the wilder highways and byways of the sunshine state.

Carl Hiaasen was born and raised in Florida and, as an investigative reporter, he made his name uncovering the kind of chicanery and corruption that fuels the plots of his distinctively offbeat and blackly comic fiction. His novels make some gestures towards providing a mystery plot which gathers momentum until the villain or villains are revealed but it is fair to say that neither the author nor his readers are as interested in the twists and turns of narrative as they are in outrageous incident and bizarre characterization. It is no accident that Hiaasen's best-known character, who was yet to make his debut in *Tourist Season* but appears in several later novels, is Skink, a former governor of Florida who has wearied of the compromises and dishonesty of politics and has retired to the wilderness to live off fresh roadkill and to wage his own one-man war against the modern world. In Hiaasen's over-the-top fiction, Skink (real name Clinton Tyree) seems entirely at home. *Tourist Season* and the novels that have followed it are full of absurd scenarios, bizarre villains and even more outlandish heroes. And beneath the mayhem, violence and dark farce, the author's serious environmental concerns are always apparent.

## ≋ Read on

*Double Whammy*; *Native Tongue*; *Sick Puppy*
Edna Buchanan, *Contents Under Pressure*; **»** James W. Hall, *Gone Wild*;
Laurence Shames, *Sunburn*

## READ ON A THEME: COMIC CAPERS

Kyril Bonfiglioli, *Don't Point That Thing at Me*
Christopher Brookmyre, *One Fine Day in the Middle of the Night*
Janet Evanovich, *Two for the Dough*
Kinky Friedman, *Greenwich Killing Time*
Peter Guttridge, *No Laughing Matter*
Sparkle Hayter, *What's a Girl Gotta Do?*
» Joe R. Lansdale, *Bad Chili*
Jonathan Latimer, *Headed for a Hearse*
» Elmore Leonard, *Be Cool*
Donald E. Westlake, *The Fugitive Pigeon*

## GEORGE V. HIGGINS (1939–99) USA

## THE FRIENDS OF EDDIE COYLE (1972)

After working as a journalist, then training as a lawyer, Boston-born Higgins became a government prosecutor, serving for seven years in cases against organized crime, including a stint as the assistant attorney for Massachusetts. He penned his first novel, *The Friends of Eddie Coyle*, in 1972 – it was highly successful and was filmed starring Robert Mitchum in the title role. A master at evoking the gritty and entirely credible world of small-time career criminals, Higgins was also wonderfully adept at naturalistic dialogue. Intriguingly, as well as being a highlight in virtually all his books, it also served to establish both plot and character and added to the books' edgy authenticity. Compelling, if often morose, the novels portrayed a drab and desperate world, successfully de-mythologizing the genre. Here, there are no dashing private eyes, with gun in hand, quip on lips and blonde on arm, but just motley bunches of criminals; men devoid of glamour, resigned to making mistakes and getting caught, as they struggle to survive in the harsh life that they have chosen, or that fate has dealt them.

The eponymous protagonist of Higgins's debut novel, Eddie 'Fingers' Coyle earned his sobriquet after having his hands slammed in a drawer and all his fingers broken. Coyle is now working for a hood named Jimmy Scalsi, selling guns to bank robbers, mobsters, revolutionaries and Black Panthers. But he is only a link in a chain and when a cop named Foley wants Scalsi, he decides to lean on Eddie, who finds himself being squeezed out of a game that was already pretty dangerous, and by some friends who really might be worse than enemies. Utterly convincing in its depiction of a very harsh reality, this is a book that is as accurate as it is suspenseful.

**Film version:** *The Friends of Eddie Coyle* (1973)

## Read on

*Impostors*; *Outlaws*; *Wonderful Years, Wonderful Years*
» K.C. Constantine, *Blood Mud*; Eugene Izzi, *Tribal Secrets*; William Lashner, *Hostile Witness*; » Elmore Leonard, *Riding the Rap*; Richard Price, *Clockers*

# PATRICIA HIGHSMITH (1921–95) USA

## THE TALENTED MR RIPLEY (1955)

Patricia Highsmith's first novel was *Strangers on a Train*, published in 1950, the story of a man lured into a bizarre plot to 'swap' murders by a man he meets on a train journey. It was made into a film by Alfred Hitchcock the following year and her later novels show that she shared the film-maker's taste for dark irony blended with psychological suspense. Her most famous character, the amoral, leisure-loving socio-path Tom Ripley, made his first appearance five years after the publication of *Strangers on a Train*, in *The Talented Mr. Ripley*. Sent to Italy by wealthy businessman Herbert Greenleaf in order to persuade Greenleaf's son Dickie to leave behind a life of *dolce far niente* on the Mediterranean and shoulder his responsibilities in New York, Ripley finds himself seduced by the idea that he could enjoy a similar life of idle indulgence. The only obstacle is Dickie. Ripley murders the young man and assumes his identity. When one of Dickie's old friends arrives in Rome, threatening to expose Ripley's crime, he is also killed. As the Italian police begin to suspect that something is amiss, Ripley re-adopts his own identity and spins his own story of what happened to Greenleaf. In the novel's ironic conclusion, the victim's father and girlfriend, and the authorities, appear to accept Ripley's version of events and he is all set to prove that crime can pay. Ripley, who appeared in several later novels by Highsmith, is one of the most memorable and disconcerting characters in all of crime fiction. Completely egotistical and willing to commit any crime to maintain the way of life he believes he deserves, he none the less engages readers' sympathies. We see everything through his eyes and, such is Highsmith's skill, we find ourselves in the unsettling position of rooting for a character who is a cold-blooded, multiple murderer.

**⛴ Film versions:** *Plein Soleil* (1960); *The Talented Mr Ripley* (1999)

**⮒ Read on**

*Ripley's Game* (the best of the Ripley sequels); *Strangers on a Train* **»** P.D. James, *The Skull Beneath the Skin*; **»** Margaret Millar, *Beast in View*

# REGINALD HILL (b. 1936) UK

## DIALOGUES OF THE DEAD (2002)

The two central characters in Hill's best-known series of crime novels – the brusque, aggressive but shrewd Superintendent Andy Dalziel and the intelligent and sensitive Chief Inspector Peter Pascoe of the Mid-Yorkshire police – first appeared in *A Clubbable Woman*, published in 1970. By the time *Dialogues of the Dead* was published, the two characters had had plenty of time and many novels in which to develop into one of the best and most entertaining double acts in contemporary English crime fiction. As the series has progressed, Hill has also become more and more ambitious, constructing ever more complex and subtle narratives of murder and mystery. In *Dialogues of the Dead* he skilfully weaves together Dalziel and Pascoe's investigations and the inner world of the killer, a word-obsessed maniac intent on playing games with the police. Two deaths that have been catalogued as accidents by the Mid-Yorkshire police have to be re-examined when stories submitted to a local library's short-story competition are found to contain details which could not have been known to anyone not involved in them. More deaths follow, all of them prefigured in the stories written by the killer the police dub 'The Wordman'. His own words become the evidence which Dalziel and Pascoe must sift and analyse and interpret in order to find out the truth. Only by solving the paper puzzles he presents can they make progress. All Reginald Hill's fiction has demonstrated his love of word games, literary allusions and the playing of sly tricks on the reader. *Dialogues of the Dead* takes that love and places it at the heart of the novel's plot. The result is his most satisfying book so far, a sophisticated, multi-layered narrative in which the two detectives and the killer, all of them caught in a web of words, battle to see who is the smartest.

## ⮂ **Read on**

*Bones and Silence*; *Death's Jest Book*; *On Beulah Height*
Stephen Booth, *Black Dog*; Graham Hurley, *Turnstone*; Val McDermid,
*A Place of Execution*; **»** Peter Robinson, *In a Dry Season*

# TONY HILLERMAN (b. 1925) USA

## A THIEF OF TIME (1988)

Among the most original crime stories of the last thirty years, Tony Hillerman's novels featuring one or both of his two Navajo tribal policemen are wholly convincing in their re-creation of a culture in which values are very different from those of the American society surrounding it. Joe Leaphorn, the older of the two men, is caught between respect for the old Navajo ways and the scepticism he has learned as he has made his way in the white world; the younger Jim Chee is, paradoxically, the one more open to the shamanism and ceremony of the past.

*A Thief of Time* begins with the disappearance of an anthropologist who has been conducting her own private investigations into the scattered archaeological sites of the long-gone Anasazi peoples in the deserts and mountains of the American South West. Leaphorn, grieving for the death of his wife and about to retire from the Navajo police, is drawn into the search for the missing woman. Meanwhile, Chee stumbles across the corpses of two 'thieves of time', pothunters and artefact-seekers who desecrate sacred ground in their search for profits. The dead thieves appear to have been involved in a larger plot to dig up and sell archaeological treasures on the black market. Leaphorn and Chee join forces as it becomes clear that not only are the cases on which they are working connected but that there are some further links with a series of horrific killings from the past. Brilliantly paced and superbly constructed, *A Thief of Time*, like Hillerman's other novels, is memorable not only for its suspense and mystery but for the skill with which he evokes the bleak beauty of the landscape in which his story is set and the culture from which his two protagonists, in different ways, take their strength.

## ⮌ Read on

*The Fallen Man*; *The Ghostway*; *People of Darkness*; *Skinwalkers*
Nevada Barr, *Track of the Cat*; James D. Doss, *The Shaman Sings*;
Marcia Muller, *Listen to the Silence*; Dana Stabenow, *A Cold Day for Murder*

# CHESTER HIMES (1909–84) USA

## A RAGE IN HARLEM (1957)

A pioneer Afro-American crime writer, Himes's drift into the underworld that he would portray so brilliantly began when he was expelled from Ohio State University for taking fellow students to one of the gambling houses he favoured. Graduating from studying to running errands for hustlers and pimps, he had numerous brushes with the law until, aged only nineteen, he was arrested for armed robbery and sentenced to 25 years. He began writing inside, publishing stories, including one in 1934 for the prestigious *Esquire* magazine, using his prison number as a byline. In 1936 he was paroled and in 1945 wrote his first novel, the critically acclaimed *If He Hollers Let Him Go*. He relocated to France in 1953, where he remained until his death. Encouraged by his French publisher, he began writing crime novels, and *A Rage in Harlem*, the first of nine, won the Grand Prix de Littérature Policière in 1958.

What Himes called his 'domestic thrillers' featured a unique double act in Coffin Ed Johnson and Grave Digger Jones, two of Harlem's toughest, orneriest cops, whose hilarious, mordant humour helped to illustrate the garish and often grotesque experience of being black in America. In their debut, they are after a gang of conmen wanted for murder in Mississippi and who have fleeced the amazingly square and naive Jackson out of his savings. Enlisting the help of his streetwise twin brother, Goldy, Jackson tries to retrieve his money and also save his beautiful girlfriend, Imabelle, who has been running with a bad crowd. Coffin Ed and Grave Digger use the twins to corner the gang but, before long, all hell breaks loose, unleashing much mayhem and violence. Beautifully written and pounding with excitement, this is the uproarious opening salvo of a marvellous series, one that is as original as it is irresistible.

**Film version:** *A Rage in Harlem* (1991)

## Read on

*Cotton Comes to Harlem*; *The Real Cool Killers*
Donald Goines, *Street Players*; **»** Walter Mosley, *Devil in a Blue Dress*; Gary Phillips, *Violent Spring*; James Sallis, *The Long-Legged Fly*; Iceberg Slim, *Mama Black Widow*

## CRAIG HOLDEN USA

### FOUR CORNERS OF NIGHT (1999)

Born in Toledo, Ohio, Holden has written five novels, each featuring different protagonists and all varied in style and subject matter. His first, *The River Sorrow*, was published in 1995 and made use of Holden's experiences as a lab technician at a medical centre. It is the powerful story of Dr Adrian Lancaster, whose dark past, including heroin addiction and obsessive love for a *femme fatale*, seemingly returns to haunt him. Holden is highly adept at employing classic *noir* plot devices to kickstart his books, a technique that is impressively used in his second novel, *The Last Sanctuary*. A Gulf War veteran is searching for his brother when he accepts a ride from a couple and gets involved with a Waco-like cult. Before long, he is wanted for robbery and murder, criss-crossing the country and pursued by the FBI, cult members and the Canadian Mounties. Holden's fourth novel is a gripping fictional account of a real event: the 1920s' murder trial of notorious bootlegger George Remus, who shot his beautiful young wife. His next, *The Narcissist's Daughter*, returns to the medical world in its masterful and chilling portrayal of two families from different sides of the tracks, as a respected, wealthy doctor takes on a streetwise student as his mentor, swiftly unleashing illicit passions and tragedy.

Holden's best novel is his third, 1999's *Four Corners of Night*, in which another *noir* trick is pulled off as the past comes back to torment two cops – best friends – when a radio call about a missing teenage girl triggers off still-simmering memories for one of them, whose daughter vanished seven years ago. Intricately structured, unbelievably dark and shocking in its depiction of clandestine desires and actions too heinous to stay hidden, this is also a perceptive and highly arresting novel, graced with exemplary characterization and busting with finely honed suspense.

### ⮷ Read on
*The River Sorrow*; *The Jazz Bird* (an historical novel based on a real-life murder case of the 1920s)
Lee Child, *Killing Floor*; David Hunt, *The Magician's Tale*

## FERGUS HUME (1859–1932) UK/Australia

### THE MYSTERY OF A HANSOM CAB (1886)

If one of » Sir Arthur Conan Doyle's Sherlock Holmes adventures had been neglected and disappeared from print, there would be an enormous outcry from aggrieved fans of the deerstalker-clad detective, yet this sad fate is precisely what befell Fergus Hume and his bestselling novel, *The Mystery of a Hansom Cab*. Published obscurely in Melbourne in 1886, a year before the first Holmes adventure (*A Study in Scarlet*), Hume's novel swiftly appeared in England and America, and became such a massive success, it was the bestselling mystery novel of the nineteenth century, reaching more readers than Holmes and his ilk.

A barrister's clerk intent on becoming a dramatist, Hume was unable to interest theatre owners in his work, and decided to publish a novel, for the express purpose of attracting local attention. Ascertaining that the mysteries of Emile Gaboriau were extremely popular, he read several and decided to write something similar; the result was this forgotten classic, a book whose immortality would doubtless be assured were its author English, American or European. Set in the dark and dangerous streets of Melbourne, the novel opens with a cabby discovering that his passenger, a very drunk man, has been murdered, a chloroform-soaked handkerchief covering his mouth. Another passenger, possibly the killer, has vanished, his identity unknown, as is that of the victim, making this impenetrable puzzle difficult for police detective Samuel Gorby to solve. In fact, he cannot unravel its myriad layers and the mystery is explained by another man, who must negotiate Melbourne's mean streets, digging up various secrets, searching for assorted papers and witnesses that both go astray and running into blackmail and, of course, murder. Rich in characters, wonderfully atmospheric and a true original, Hume's book has, despite its current obscurity, been widely acknowledged to be among the hundred best crime novels. Find out why.

## ⮂ Read on

*The Green Mummy*; *Madame Midas*

Charles Dickens, *The Mystery of Edwin Drood*; **»** Sir Arthur Conan Doyle, *The Sign of Four*; Emile Gaboriau, *The Mystery of Orcival*

# FRANCIS ILES (1893–1971) UK

## MALICE AFORETHOUGHT (1931)

Narrated by a small-town doctor named Bickleigh, *Malice Afore-thought* is a powerful portrait of a mind slowly disintegrating under intolerable stress. Bickleigh is trapped in an unhappy marriage, and his misery leads him inexorably from flirtation to a love affair and from adultery to what he believes, mistakenly, to be the perfect murder. There is no mystery in *Malice Aforethought* to tempt the reader's interest. From the novel's earliest pages, we know the perpetrator of the crime and, to some extent, his motives for committing it. Iles assumes, rightly, that his readers will be as interested in seeing, from the inside, the slow progression of Bickleigh's mental deterioration as in solving the kind of puzzle that detective novels of the era usually presented. Set in a claustrophobic society where snobbery is rampant (Bickleigh's wife believes that she has married beneath her and loses no opportunity of letting her husband know this), *Malice Aforethought* works so well because it allows readers to understand, and indeed sympathize, with a man driven to murder by the sense that his life has become a prison and he has only one chance of escape.

Francis Iles was one of the pseudonyms of Anthony Berkeley Cox who, as Anthony Berkeley, wrote a series of English detective novels featuring an amateur sleuth and crime novelist called Roger Shering-ham. The self-satisfied and nosy Sheringham is the occasionally irritating hero of books which work as both affectionate parodies and ideal exemplars of the standard detective novel of the inter-war years. In *Malice Aforethought*, Berkeley Cox produced a very different kind of book – one which pioneered the kind of psychological crime story now practised by so many writers, from **»** Ruth Rendell to **»** Minette Walters. More than seventy years after its first publication, it remains a highly original and absorbing novel.

**Film versions:** *Malice Aforethought* (TV 1979); *Malice Aforethought* (TV 2005)

**Read on**
*Before the Fact*; *As for the Woman* (the two other novels written as Francis Iles); *The Poisoned Chocolates Case* (the best of the Roger Sheringham stories)
C.S. Forester, *Payment Deferred*


# MICHAEL INNES (1906–94) UK

## HAMLET, REVENGE! (1937)
For 50 years, the Oxford don J.I.M. Stewart used the pseudonym Michael Innes to publish a series of self-consciously erudite, whimsical crime stories, crammed with literary allusions and quotations and featuring the urbane and intelligent police inspector, John Appleby. The best of the series, *Hamlet, Revenge!*, is set, like so many novels from the Golden Age of English detective fiction, against the backdrop of a country house party. During the party, an amateur production of Hamlet

is staged and, at the moment Polonius is due to be stabbed behind the arras, the actor playing him, a political high-flyer named Lord Auldearn, is shot dead. Inspector Appleby finds himself pursuing the murderer down the corridors of power and looking for his suspects among the great and the good of the land.

The critic and novelist » Julian Symons once described what he called the 'farceur' school of English detective fiction. Michael Innes is the prime example of this school. His novels do not ask to be taken too seriously and they draw flamboyant attention to their unlikely characters and incredible plots. In *Appleby's End*, for example, the detective inspector unexpectedly becomes the guest of a bizarre family, descended from a minor Victorian Gothic novelist named Ranulph Raven, who are being plagued by mysterious events which seem to echo their ancestor's books. Farm animals are replaced by marble effigies; one member of the family receives a tombstone with his own name and death date on it; a servant is found dead, buried up to his neck in a snow-filled field. No one should pick up a Michael Innes novel expecting social realism or mean streets but, in books like *Hamlet, Revenge!* and *Appleby's End*, he did create his own unmistakable world in which to unfold his fantastic and often farcical plots.

## ⮂ Read on

*Appleby's End*; *Death at the President's Lodging*
» Edmund Crispin, *Buried for Pleasure*; Robert Robinson, *Landscape With Dead Dons*

# P.D. JAMES (b. 1920) UK

## A TASTE FOR DEATH (1986)

Two bodies are found in the vestry of a London church, their throats cut. One is a tramp who had regularly used church premises as a doss-house. The other is a prominent Tory MP, Sir Paul Berowne. As P.D. James's sensitive and intelligent detective, the poet and police-man Adam Dalgliesh, investigates the mystery of what led two such different men to be united in death, he is drawn further and further into the tangled lives of Berowne's family and friends. Beneath a veneer of gentility and old-world politesse, the Berownes and their associates have plenty to hide and it becomes Dalgliesh's job to bring secrets to light and to decide which, if any, are relevant to his enquiries.

In many ways, the novels of P.D. James are throwbacks to the Golden Age of classic English crime fiction. They take place in settings where » Dorothy L. Sayers's Lord Peter Wimsey would not have been out of place. In *Death in Holy Orders*, Dalgliesh visits St Anselm's, an isolated theological college on the Norfolk coast which is thrown into turmoil by a grisly and sacrilegious murder in its chapel; in *Original Sin*, an old-fashioned gentlemanly publishing firm is disturbed by the killing of its managing director. The sensitive and humane Dalgliesh has more in common with the amateur detectives of past eras than the streetwise coppers of today's crime fiction. Yet James's books do not share the unthreatening cosiness that characterizes so many of the novels of the Golden Age. The crimes they describe in unflinching detail are brutal and bloody, the threats to the social order they represent are very real. In long, leisurely yet utterly gripping narratives like *A Taste for Death*, P.D. James combines all the virtues of the classic English detective story with a psychological realism and an awareness of the disruptive power of violence that is entirely contemporary.

### ⮒ Read on

*An Unsuitable Job for a Woman*; *A Certain Justice*; *Death in Holy Orders*; *Original Sin* (which introduces James's other series character, the young female private investigator Cordelia Gray)

Gwendoline Butler, *A Dark Coffin*; Caroline Graham, *The Killings at Badger's Drift*; Janet Neel, *Death's Bright Angel*; » Dorothy L. Sayers, *The Nine Tailors*

# STUART M. KAMINSKY (b. 1934) USA

## MURDER ON THE YELLOW BRICK ROAD (1977)

Kaminsky has written over 50 novels, four biographies and numerous books on cinema and television, but it is his series featuring detective Toby Peters that has won the greatest acclaim. Set in a warmly depicted 1930s' and '40s' Los Angeles, the books are a delight for crime fans and movie buffs alike. As well as penning fine mysteries, Kaminsky has effectively fashioned an alternative portrayal of Hollywood at its peak, during a golden period when the stars ruled the world and the studios ruled the stars. Central to the books is Toby Peters, an amiable down-at-heel private eye, who is assisted by a varied and richly comic supporting cast including his waitress girlfriend Anita, Sheldon Minck, a myopic dentist with whom he shares an office and, crucially, his elder brother Phil, a bad-tempered police officer who alternates between bailing Toby out of trouble and hitting him. Alongside this disparate bunch are some of the silver screen's biggest names: Fred Astaire, Charlie Chaplin, Joan Crawford, Bette Davis, Errol Flynn, Cary Grant, Bela Lugosi, Mae West and many others, who all play second fiddle to Toby's unassuming, ironic lead.

Opening with the classic line, 'Someone had murdered a Munchkin', the second novel, *Murder on the Yellow Brick Road*, finds the detective investigating the suspicious death of a cast member of *The Wizard of Oz*, a year after the film's successful release. Rubbing shoulders with a frail Judy Garland and MGM's boss, the considerably more robust Louis B. Mayer – the real wizard here – Toby has to think fast to outwit a killer who is stalking the studio's backlots. A romantic entanglement, a friendship with another Munchkin and notable cameos from Clark Gable, Mickey Rooney and an obscure writer called **»** Raymond Chandler only add to the excitement as the battered sleuth heads over the rainbow and emerges triumphant.

## ⮂ Read on

*Dancing in the Dark*; *The Howard Hughes Affair*; *Mildred Pierced*; *Never Cross a Vampire*; *A Cold Red Sunrise* (one of the best of Kaminsky's Inspector Rostnikov mysteries which feature a maverick Russian detective)

W.T. Ballard, *Hollywood Troubleshooter*; George Baxt, *The William Powell and Myrna Loy Murder Case*

## READ**ON**A**THEME:** TINSELTOWN CRIME

Andrew Bergman, *Hollywood and Levine*
Anthony Boucher, *The Case of the Baker Street Irregulars*
» Raymond Chandler, *The Little Sister*
Tim Dorsey, *The Big Bamboo*
Terence Faherty, *Come Back Dead*
» Robert Ferrigno, *Scavenger Hunt*
David Handler, *The Boy Who Never Grew Up*
Jonathan Latimer, *Black is the Fashion for Dying*
» Elmore Leonard, *Get Shorty*
Jay Russell, *Greed and Stuff*

# JOE R. LANSDALE (b. 1951) USA

## THE BOTTOMS (2000)

Joe Lansdale is best known for his series of violently farcical novels in which Hap Collins, white and straight, and Leonard Pine, black and gay, join forces in an odd crime team let loose among the rednecks of the Deep South, but *The Bottoms* is something very different. Deftly combining a murder mystery with an elegiac coming-of-age story, the book is set in east Texas in the mid-1930s when its narrator, Harry Crane, is on the verge of his teenage years. Harry is brutally exposed to the realities of the adult world when he discovers a mutilated body, bound with barbed wire to a tree in the river bottoms near his home. While his father, the local constable, searches for the killer and racial tensions explode in further violence, Harry and his younger sister, Thomasina (Tom), speculate that the killer is the Goat Man, a bogeyman of local legend who is said to haunt the woods and riverbanks of the neighbourhood. Harry and Tom believe that they have seen the Goat Man and their curiosity about the supposed monster leads them both into dangers that they cannot fully understand.

Unlike the over-the-top, pulp adventures of Hap Collins and Leonard Pine, *The Bottoms* is a novel that quietly but relentlessly builds up suspense and tension as readers begin to realize that Harry and Tom face threats far worse than any posed by the supposed Goat Man. People in the real world are far more scary than any bogeyman of their childish imaginings. The years of the Great Depression and its effects on the lives of the Cranes are beautifully evoked in a restrained prose that owes little to Lansdale's earlier, more rumbustious writing and the story develops into a remarkably powerful portrait of a small, rural community descending into fear and paranoia.

## ≋ Read on

*The Two-Bear Mambo*; *Mucho Mojo* (the earliest and best of the series featuring Lansdale's odd couple, Hap Collins and Leonard Pine)
Stephen Dobyns, *The Church of Dead Girls*; Sharyn McCrumb, *The Hangman's Beautiful Daughter*

# DENNIS LEHANE (b. 1966) USA

## MYSTIC RIVER (2001)

Lehane was born and lives in Dorchester, Massachusetts, and is the author of seven crime novels, set in or around his native town and the Boston area. The first five feature private investigators and erstwhile lovers Patrick Kenzie and Angela Gennaro, along with their sidekick and hired muscle, the larger-than-life Bubba Rogowski. Set in largely blue-collar, often American-Irish areas of Boston, the books' colourful humour and razor-sharp wisecracks do not disguise the fact that they probe the darkest corners of the human condition. Several of them feature child abuse as a theme and the domestic violence running through them seems so common as to be almost casual or expected. Childhood friends, briefly involved and professional partners for years, Kenzie and Gennaro make a compelling and entertaining double act as they run their investigation agency from the belfry of a Boston church. But as Patrick still bears the emotional scars inflicted by his father, a firefighter who terrorized his family, and since Angie has struggled to escape her abusive husband, both of them have an intimate knowledge of domestic brutality.

Lehane has also written two stand-alone novels, *Mystic River* and *Shutter Island*. Both were highly successful, but his reputation really took off when the first of these became a bestseller and subsequently hit the big screen, directed and produced by Clint Eastwood. It is the grim, but entirely compelling story about three friends, Dave Boyle, Sean Devine and Jimmy Marcus, and of something that happened twenty-five years ago to all of them, but specifically to Dave; something so terrible that it sundered their friendship. When Jimmy's daughter is murdered, the three men, on different sides of the law now, are united once more and each has to face again the evil that separated them all those years ago.

🎬 **Film version:** *Mystic River* (2003)

🔖 **Read on**
*Darkness, Take My Hand*; *A Drink Before the War*; *Gone, Baby, Gone*; *Prayers for Rain*; *Sacred* (all Kenzie and Gennaro novels); *Shutter Island*
Richard Barre, *The Innocents*; » Harlan Coben, *One False Move*; » K.C. Constantine, *The Man Who Liked to Look at Himself*

# DONNA LEON (b. 1942) USA

## DEATH IN A STRANGE COUNTRY (1993)
A body is pulled out of a Venetian canal and proves to be that of a young American soldier from a base in the hills of the Veneto. Is he the victim of a casual mugging or is there an even more sinister explanation for his death? Commissario Brunetti, the protagonist in all Leon's Venetian tales, finds that his enquiries are leading him inexorably towards dirty linen that few people want to wash in public. Drugs are found in the young man's flat but they may have been planted there to divert attention from other lines of investigation that Brunetti might

wish to pursue. Very powerful people indeed have a vested interest in ensuring that the truth about the American's death, and others that follow, should never emerge.

The two great strengths of Donna Leon's splendid series of novels set in Venice are her portrait of the city itself and her creation of Commissario Brunetti. Leon's Venice is not a sentimentalized vision of 'the Pearl of the Adriatic' but a city in which drugs, prostitution and corruption lurk in the shadows. The thoughtful and humane Brunetti moves through its *calli* and *campi* with an honest determination to get at as much of the truth as he can but he is only too aware that powers beyond his own are often at work. The Commissario is a rounded and convincing character in a way that few others in contemporary crime fiction are. We see him not only as a professional law officer but as a family man, devoted to his wife Paola and his two children. We share his rueful appreciation that might will usually triumph over right, especially if his superior officer, Patta, a man whose interest lies more in ingratiating himself with the powers that be than in solving crimes, is involved. In ***Death in a Strange Country***, as in Leon's other novels, we are brilliantly drawn into Brunetti's world and the city which he loves.

## ‿ Read on

*Death at La Fenice*; *A Noble Radiance*; *Fatal Remedies*
Michael Dibdin, ***Vendetta***; David Hewson, ***A Season for the Dead***; Timothy Holme, ***The Devil and the Dolce Vita***; Magdalen Nabb, ***The Marshal and the Murderer***

## READONATHEME: CRIMES AROUND THE WORLD

Aaron Elkins, *Twenty Blue Devils* (Tahiti)
Dan Fesperman, *Lie in the Dark* (Bosnia)
» Tony Hillerman, *Finding Moon* (Cambodia)
Peter Hoeg, *Miss Smilla's Feeling for Snow* (Greenland)
Alexander McCall Smith, *The No. 1 Ladies' Detective Agency* (Botswana)
James McClure, *The Steam Pig* (South Africa)
Sujata Massey, *The Samurai's Daughter* (Japan)
Eliot Pattison, *The Skull Mantra* (Tibet)
Charles Powers, *In the Memory of the Forest* (Poland)
Martin Cruz Smith, *Gorky Park* (Russia)

# ELMORE LEONARD (b. 1925) USA

## LA BRAVA (1983)

Born in New Orleans, Leonard moved to Detroit when he was ten, later serving in the navy and studying English literature at university. Working as an advertising copywriter, he also began writing stories and novels, mainly westerns, for pulp magazines and paperback publishers. After selling his novel, *Hombre*, to Hollywood in 1966, he wrote full-time, knocking out thrillers and westerns. In the 1970s, he began to write a number of fast-paced crime novels, set in Detroit and Florida, each one graced with brilliant dialogue and memorable one-word titles. *Swag*, *Stick*, *Bandits* and *Glitz* were bestsellers and some were filmed. Reaching his fifties, he had finally arrived and, inspired to prolificacy, produced a steady stream of successful and influential crime novels, many of which became hit movies, such as *Out of Sight*, *Get Shorty* and *Rum Punch* (filmed as *Jackie Brown* by Quentin Tarantino, an avowed fan).

In 1983, in the midst of this wave of success, he wrote *La Brava*, something of a departure in that it is more thoughtful than its slam-bang neighbours, and its protagonist, Joe La Brava, a former Secret Service agent turned photographer, is more likeable than most of Leonard's characters, who are often riven by conflict and brimming with bad attitude. Joe meets Jean Shaw, a former movie star on whom he used to have an adolescent crush, but who is now a heavy drinking, fadingly beautiful woman living out a strange twilight existence. As she is apparently being dragged into an extortion scheme and needs his help, he is happy to oblige. With a cast of typical Leonard characters, such as a redneck former cop who bristles with menace and a murderous, go-go dancing Cuban refugee, *La Brava* may or may not be the best of Leonard's many books, but it is certainly up there near the top.

## ⮒ Read on

*Freaky Deaky*; *Get Shorty*; *Rum Punch*

» Loren D. Estleman, *Motor City Blue*; Laurence Shames, *Florida Straits*; Don Winslow, *California Fire and Life*

# GASTON LEROUX (1868–1927) France

## THE MYSTERY OF THE YELLOW ROOM (1907)

Best known as the writer who originally created the haunting figure of the Phantom of the Opera, Gaston Leroux also published a sequence of mystery novels featuring the teenage amateur detective Rouletabille. The first of these, *The Mystery of the Yellow Room*, remains one of the greatest of all 'locked room' mysteries. Professor Stangerson is a Franco-American scientist of great renown who has retired to an isolated chateau outside Paris to work on his potentially world-changing experiments. Living with him is his daughter, about to be married after a long courtship to another scientist. One night, as the professor is working late, his daughter retires to her room, the yellow room of the title. Suddenly, awful cries of 'Murder – murder – help' are heard coming from the room. When the professor and his servants break into it, they find Mlle Stangerson lying on the floor, terribly injured and unable to speak. The door to the room was locked from the inside; so too were the metal blinds on its only window. The assailant seems to have disappeared into thin air and there is talk among the servants that the Devil has been at work in the chateau. It is up to the crime reporter Rouletabille to throw light on the mystery of what has happened to Mlle Stangerson. Like a much younger, smarter, French brother of Sherlock Holmes, Rouletabille spots clues that everyone else has missed, makes deductive leaps no one else is imaginative enough to contemplate and throws out cryptic remarks to his Dr Watson, the lawyer Sainclair, which go to the heart of the puzzle. *The Mystery of the Yellow Room*, like the Holmes' stories, is a product of its era but it is much more than just a period piece. Leroux manipulates his plot with great skill, from the first exposition of the mystery to the dramatic denouement, and, in the precocious Rouletabille, a master detective who has scarcely started shaving, he creates a memorable central character.

🕮 **Film version:** *Le Mystère de la Chambre Jaune* (1949); *Le Mystère de la Chambre Jaune* (2003)

≋ **Read on**
*The Phantom of the Opera*
» John Dickson Carr, *It Walks by Night*; Israel Zangwill, *The Big Bow Mystery*

# ED MCBAIN (1926–2005) USA

## SADIE WHEN SHE DIED (1972)
Salvatore Albert Lombino was born in New York City, and after serving in the navy and then working as a teacher, began writing full time, legally changing his name on his agent's advice and swiftly becoming so prolific that he wrote under several labels; the most famous being Evan Hunter and Ed McBain. As Hunter, his most celebrated book was his third novel, *The Blackboard Jungle*, published in 1954. Based on his own experiences as a teacher at an inner city school, it was filmed a year later, and with Bill Haley's song *Rock Around the Clock* playing

over the credits, helped to usher in the age of rock'n'roll. As McBain, he wrote over fifty novels set in the 87th Precinct of a fictional city, called Isola, generally acknowledged to be New York. This finely-honed series of police procedural stories featured a lively cast headed by detective Steve Carella, and was originally dreamed up when the publishers, Pocket Books, anxious about the advancing years of **»** Erle Stanley Gardner, creator of Perry Mason, wanted both a new mystery series and a new author.

*Sadie When She Died* was the 26th book in the series, and found Carella investigating the death of beautiful Sarah Fletcher, fatally stabbed during a bungled burglary. Despite having a confession, convenient fingerprints and a witness's report, Carella is not happy, especially when the husband, a criminal lawyer, expresses pleasure at his wife's violent death. He is even more suspicious when his sleuthing turns up the woman's little black book, which happens to contain a very long list of her clandestine trysts. Aided by his fellow officer Bert Kling, Carella is soon combing the city's seamier spots, probing its sexual secrets, trying to find the real killer and seeing if he can discover why the men called Sarah Fletcher Sadie when she died.

## ⮒ Read on

*Cop Killer*; *Eighty Million Eyes*; *Fuzz*; *Hail, Hail, the Gang's All Here*; *Killer's Choice* (all 87th Precinct novels); *The House That Jack Built* (one of McBain's non-87th Precinct series featuring the Florida-based attorney and detective Matthew Hope)

William Caunitz, *One Police Plaza*; Eugene Izzi, *Bad Guys*; **»** Joseph Wambaugh, *The Choirboys*

## READONATHEME: PROCEDURALS
## (AMERICAN)

» Michael Connelly, *Angels Flight*
  W.E.B. Griffin, *The Investigators*
  Tami Hoag, *Dust to Dust*
  J.A. Jance, *Name Withheld*
» Stuart M. Kaminsky, *Lieberman's Law*
  Faye Kellerman, *Prayers for the Dead*
  Carol O'Connell, *Crime School*
» Joseph Wambaugh, *Finnegan's Week*
  Hillary Waugh, *Last Seen Wearing*

## CAMERON MCCABE (1915–95) Germany

THE FACE ON THE CUTTING ROOM FLOOR (1937)

This is one of those rare books wherein the mystery found in its pages may well be less significant that the one attached to its origins. Author and critic » Julian Symons famously observed that it was a 'dazzling... unrepeatable box of tricks', while poet and critic Sir Herbert Read succinctly if puzzlingly described it as 'Hegelian'. On publication, the book was credited to Cameron McCabe, a busy fellow since he also serves as the protagonist and narrator, dishing up a bizarre tale of a young actress whose body is discovered on the cutting room floor of a London film studio, and who is later joined by her ex-lover, a Norwegian actor, who is found with a nasty bullet hole in his head.

Film editor McCabe tells the story as if he is reading a pastiche of an American crime novel, but translated by a drunken Surrealist. Flicking out details like cigarette ash, he challenges the reader to keep up as he dashes frantically around the city on the trail of a killer, racing from the studio in King's Cross towards the West India Dock Road, then around Holborn, Fleet Street, everywhere, in fact. Viewed from his warped perspective, London has never seemed so alien. Just to keep things from becoming too cosy, he also engages in a complex and torrid love triangle and a battle of wits with Scotland Yard's Detective Inspector Smith, where roles are reversed, then apparently reversed again.

Decades later, the real author was revealed as Ernest Julius Borneman, a young refugee from Nazi Germany with an eccentric command of English, which may explain the novel's unusual narrative, and who later became a noted sexologist, which may explain the love triangle. Utterly unique, this is a truly haunting book that, once read, is not easily forgotten.

## ⮂ Read on

Marc Behm, *The Eye of the Beholder*; Eric Garcia, *Anonymous Rex*; William Hjortsberg, *Falling Angel*; Jonathan Lethem, *Gun, With Occasional Music*; Ray Vukcevich, *The Man of Maybe Half-a-Dozen Faces* (in their different ways, these novels all resemble *The Face on the Cutting Room Floor* in that they are utterly unlike any other crime fiction)

# JOHN D. MACDONALD (1916–86) USA

## THE DEEP BLUE GOODBYE (1964)

A remarkably prolific author, MacDonald wrote 78 books, as well as almost five hundred stories, in a career lasting nearly forty years. His most famous and successful books were the series of Travis McGee novels, which numbered 21. Whether he had been perfecting them by 'incubating' several books and waiting for the right time to deliver them or was just on a superhuman roll and wrote them in a single stretch, but MacDonald published the first *four* McGee novels in just one year – 1964. They were set in Florida, a place that he certainly made his own, since he was the first in a long run of authors to depict it as the day-glo demi-monde it apparently was. Novelist and celebrated sunshine statesman » Carl Hiaasen believed that MacDonald 'was the first modern writer to nail Florida dead-centre, to capture all its languid sleaze, racy sense of promise and breath-grabbing beauty'.

*The Deep Blue Goodbye* introduces a new kind of character who is neither cop nor private eye, but lives in Fort Lauderdale on a houseboat that he won in a poker game and called, appropriately, the *Busted Flush*. McGee is a 'salvage expert', which means that he finds things for people who have lost them, taking half their value in payment. A beach bum who works only when he needs to, or when doing someone a favour, he has a Zen approach to life that gives a nod to the Beat generation, but he also has a fierce sense of moral conviction. Here, he tries to retrieve the plundered inheritance of Cathy Kerr, a woman who has lost everything but her dignity. All he has to do is find out how her father made his money, catch the man who stole it and then take it back. Witty, sexy and beautifully written, the McGee books are sublime entertainment and not to be missed.

### ⮂ Read on

*A Deadly Shade of Gold*; *The Green Ripper*; *One Fearful Yellow Eye*; *The Executioners* (the novel on which the two films called *Cape Fear* were based)

» James W. Hall, *Squall*; » Carl Hiaasen, *Double Whammy*; Randy Wayne White, *Ten Thousand Islands*

# ROSS MACDONALD (1915–83) USA

## THE MOVING TARGET (1949)

Born Kenneth Millar in San Francisco, the man who later became Ross Macdonald was raised in Canada, where many of his novels' plots have their origin. A talented writer of thrillers with a striking psychological bent, the earliest of which reveal a somewhat conspicuous debt to » Raymond Chandler, Macdonald upped his game with *The Moving Target*. This, his fifth book, was the first in a series featuring private investigator Lew Archer, a tough, intelligent and likeable Los Angeles detective and, as well as being Archer's first bow, saw the author's books appearing under the byline of Ross Macdonald. Living in Santa Barbara after the war, Macdonald had plenty of opportunity to study the wayward inhabitants of southern California and he put this to excellent use, fashioning a highly perceptive portrayal of this idiosyncratic region. After ten years of perfecting his craft, using the Archer books to create substantial and dramatic studies of dysfunctional families, he wrote *The Galton Case* in 1959, a breakthrough novel and the first whose theme was the pursuit of identity, destined to be the prevalent topic in his subsequent work.

*The Moving Target* finds the private eye investigating the kidnapping of millionaire Ralph Sampson. A host of classic Californian grotesqueries emerge from the sunshine to be appraised by the shrewd sleuth, including a self-styled guru to whom Sampson has bequeathed his mountain retreat; his wife, a bitter invalid; his sultry daughter, who is being courted by both her father's young pilot and his ageing lawyer and a female jazz pianist, who is a drug addict. Although Archer is a sleeker, more upbeat version of Chandler's Philip Marlowe, and the book has many echoes of the classic *noir* works of the 1940s, it is an absolute gem and with it, Macdonald resolutely pointed the way forward for the American crime novel.

🎞 **Film version:** *Harper* (1966) Archer's character undergoes a name change for the silver screen and becomes Lew Harper in this and its sequel, *The Drowning Pool*

🔁 **Read on**
*The Goodbye Look*; *The Moving Target*; *The Underground Man*
Richard Barre, *The Ghosts of Morning*; » Raymond Chandler, *Farewell, My Lovely*; Roger L. Simon, *California Roll*; Jonathan Valin, *Day of Wrath*

# MICHAEL MALONE (b. 1942) USA

## UNCIVIL SEASONS (1983)

Author of several beautifully crafted novels and numerous television scripts, Malone has also written three excellent crime novels. Set in the fictional town of Hillston, North Carolina, they feature police officers and good friends Justin Savile V and Cuddy Mangum. Justin is the scion of the aristocratic Saviles, Hillston's founding clan, and, though he has somewhat forsaken his privileged position to become a lowly detective, he's judiciously maintained his *droit de seigneur* by being as drunk as a lord and dallying with an endless stream of ladies. From the wrong side of the tracks, Cuddy is proud of his humble origins and, through hard work and determination, rises up the ladder to become Hillston's chief of police. Even as he acquires more authority, power and official recognition, it is the charming dilettante, Justin, who seems to be the better detective.

In *Uncivil Seasons* Hillston is beset by freak blizzards, and the snow flurries cover not only the town, but also a recent brutal murder, that of wealthy Cloris Dollard, the wife of Justin's uncle. The powers that be want Justin simply to arrest the chief suspect, a scapegoat, but naturally, he prefers to do things his way. This includes listening to Joanna Cadmean, a beautiful, middle-aged mystic, whose visions seem to lead him towards the killer, and the inflammatory advice dished out by Cuddy. Justin's pursuit of the truth, a commodity deemed irrelevant by Hillston's good burghers, means asking a lot of awkward questions and his relentless probing soon starts to rattle a few of the town's gilded cages. As the movers and shakers advance to prevent him from ever moving and shaking again, he and Cuddy have to ransack the past, raking up the still-burning coals of avarice, corruption and evil, in order to confront and combat the horrors of the present.

## ➢ Read on

*First Lady*; *Time's Witness*

Dick Lochte, *Blue Bayou*; Margaret Maron, *Southern Discomfort*; Marcie Walsh and » Michael Malone, *The Killing Club*

# HENNING MANKELL (b. 1948) Sweden

## SIDETRACKED (1999)

A teenage girl commits suicide by burning herself to death. A serial killer with a taste for gruesome violence and an urge to scalp his victims is on the loose. His first victim is a former minister of justice whose mutilated body is found on the beach in a wealthy neighbourhood. Further corpses are soon found. Inspector Kurt Wallander, who has been a horrified witness to the girl's self-immolation, looks for a reason for her despair while also heading the police search for the killer. Links between the deaths prove elusive but Wallander's melancholy determination to do his job eventually leads him towards the truth.

Like Mankell's other Wallander novels, this is not a conventional mystery story. Readers know the identity of the killer well before the book's conclusion. The emphasis is not on a puzzle that needs to be worked out but on character and on the contradictions and corruption of the Swedish society in which Wallander lives. The Sweden Mankell describes is a country where the welfare-state idealism of the past has turned sour and the values of tolerance and social inclusiveness are under constant threat. Racism and violence lurk beneath the thin veneer of civilized society. Wallander, confronted by daily horrors in his job and faced by personal and family difficulties, struggles to maintain his own decency and honesty. Often haunted by the crimes he is investigating (in *Sidetracked* the image of the girl burning enters his dreams), he is an unglamorous, thoughtful but strangely compelling central character around whom Mankell has constructed some of the most memorable crime novels of recent years. Beginning with *Faceless Killers*, a story in which the murders of an elderly couple on an isolated farm become the focus of racial tensions, the Wallander novels provide an unforgiving portrait of contemporary society but one which we can all recognize.

## ≋ Read on

*The Dogs of Riga*; *Faceless Killers*

Kerstin Ekman, *Blackwater*; Karin Fossum, *Don't Look Back*; Arnaldur Indridason, *Jar City*; Maj Sjöwall and Per Wahlöö, *The Laughing Policeman*

## READONATHEME: EUROPEAN CRIME

Jakob Arjouni, *Happy Birthday, Turk*
Massimo Carlotto, *The Colombian Mule*
Eugenio Fuentes, *The Depths of the Forest*
Sebastien Japrisot, *10.30 From Marseilles*
Petros Markaris, *The Late-Night News*
Ingrid Noll, *The Pharmacist*
José Carlos Somoza, *The Art of Murder*
Gunnar Staalesen, *The Writing on the Wall*
Jan Willem van de Wetering, *Death of a Hawker*
Fred Vargas, *Seeking Whom He May Devour*

# NGAIO MARSH (1899–1982) New Zealand

## OFF WITH HIS HEAD (1957)

Regularly bracketed with » Agatha Christie and » Dorothy L. Sayers as one of the queens of English Golden Age crime fiction, Ngaio Marsh was the creator of Chief Inspector (later Superintendent) Roderick Alleyn, a cultured and urbane detective who appears in most of her fiction. Several of her best novels (*Opening Night*, *Enter a Murderer*, *Final Curtain*) are set in the world of the theatre, which she knew well and which she views with a wry affection. Others (*Surfeit of Lampreys* and *Night at the Vulcan*, for example) have naive young characters from

New Zealand, Marsh's own native country, thrown into murder mysteries when they visit London for the first time.

With the observant eye of the outsider, Marsh wrote very well about the oddities and idiosyncrasies of English life and *Off With His Head*, set in an imaginary village even weirder than such villages often are in the real world, is one of her most entertaining and enjoyable novels. In South Mardian, the ancient ritual known as the Dance of the Five Sons is performed annually at the winter solstice. A macabre mixture of Morris dance and folk play, it culminates in the symbolic decapitation of one of the dancers. When one year's ceremony ends with a beheading that is only too real and is witnessed by the assembled villagers, Inspector Alleyn faces one of his most baffling murder mysteries and is obliged to look behind the disguises and deceptions of the Dance of the Five Sons to reveal who the killer was and how he committed his apparently impossible crime. Filled with memorable characters – from Dame Alice Mardian, the formidable lady of the manor, to Mrs Bunz, the interfering German expert on European folk culture – *Off With His Head* shows all the skill in constructing an entertainingly convoluted plot that made Ngaio Marsh a rival to Christie and Sayers.

## ⮧ **Read on**
*Death and the Dancing Footman*; *Singing in the Shrouds*; *Surfeit of Lampreys*
Caroline Graham, *Death of a Hollow Man*; Martha Grimes, *I Am the Only Running Footman*; **»** Michael Innes, *Hamlet, Revenge!*

# MARGARET MILLAR (1915–94) Canada/USA

## BEAST IN VIEW (1955)

Helen Clarvoe is a reclusive young woman, terrified of the wider world outside the Hollywood residential hotel in which she lives. One day her safe but restricted life is dramatically changed when she receives an abusive telephone call from someone who claims to be an old school friend named Evelyn Merrick. Evelyn threatens her with crystal ball visions of a future in which a bleeding and mutilated Helen has suffered a terrible accident. Terrified, Helen reluctantly allows an old family friend, Paul Blackshear, to make efforts to track down the caller. As Blackshear investigates the lives of both Helen and her family and of Evelyn Merrick, he is drawn into a seedy world of extortion, drugs and pornography where little is what it seems and everyone has something to hide. Helen herself is forced to emerge from the seclusion in which she has lived and wrestle with the demons from her past.

Born in Canada, Margaret Millar spent her adult life in the USA, largely in California, and she was married to Kenneth Millar (better known, under his pseudonym **»** Ross Macdonald, as the creator of the private eye Lew Archer). Her own career as a crime writer began in the early 1940s with a series of novels featuring a psychiatrist turned detective named Paul Prye and she was still publishing in the late 1980s. *Spider Webs*, which appeared in 1986, is a gripping, often satirical courtroom thriller with a devastating twist in its tail. *Beast in View*, much acclaimed on its first publication, has long been her most famous novel. Although the passage of time has made some of its depictions of Hollywood's underbelly seem almost quaintly restrained, Millar's narrative remains exceptionally powerful and, as it moves inexorably towards a final revelation that can still shock readers, it provides clear evidence of her skill and ingenuity as a writer.

### ⮂ Read on

*Ask for Me Tomorrow*; *How Like an Angel*; *A Stranger in My Grave*
Celia Fremlin, *The Hours Before Dawn*; **»** Patricia Highsmith, *Strangers on a Train*

## GLADYS MITCHELL (1901–83) UK

### COME AWAY, DEATH (1937)

Creator of one of the most compelling characters in the Golden Age of English detective fiction, psychiatric adviser to the Home Office Dame Beatrice Lestrange Bradley, Gladys Mitchell published her idiosyncratic novels for more than half a century. She began writing at a time when Hercule Poirot was a relative newcomer to crime fiction and was still putting pen to paper in the early 1980s but her books often seem untouched by time. 'The Great Gladys', as her admirer Philip Larkin once described her, was *sui generis* and the fantastical world she created must have seemed as odd and unique in the 1930s as it does today. An English village ruled by a mad squire is beset by witchcraft (***The Devil at Saxon Wall***); a circus tight-rope walker is murdered when the moon is full (***The Rising of the Moon***); bodies are found in the River Itchen at

Winchester and rumours abound that a water nymph is luring young boys to their deaths (*Death and the Maiden*) – Gladys Mitchell's fictional world is filled with bizarre events and eccentric characters.

One of Mitchell's very finest books, *Come Away, Death* takes Dame Beatrice out of the archetypal English landscapes in which she is usually seen and places her in the blazing heat and dusty terrain of Greece. She is part of a tour group visiting ancient temples under the direction of a half-demented scholar named Sir Rudri Hopkinson, who dreams of recreating the old Greek sacrificial rituals at the sites where they were originally enacted. Strange events occur wherever the group goes, eventually culminating in murder and the discovery of a bloody head in a box of snakes, and Dame Beatrice is obliged to draw on her knowledge of both human psychology and Greek mythology to solve the crimes. Comic, unsettling and just plain weird, the novel shows why Gladys Mitchell was a crime writer unlike any other from the Golden Age.

### ≋ Read on

*Dead Men's Morris, The Rising of the Moon, The Twenty-Third Man*
» Ngaio Marsh, *Death at the Bar*; » Dorothy L. Sayers, *Five Red Herrings*

# MANUEL VÁZQUEZ MONTALBÁN

**(1939–2003)** Spain

## MURDER IN THE CENTRAL COMMITTEE (1988)

In many crime series the city in which the action takes place is as important as the detective. From Philip Marlowe's Los Angeles to John Rebus's Edinburgh, cities matter in crime fiction. Barcelona, as seen through the eyes of Pepe Carvalho, the creation of the Spanish writer Manuel Vázquez Montalbán, is as memorable a setting as any series has. Montalbán began his writing career as a dissident journalist (he was imprisoned under Franco's regime) and as a poet, but his real success began when he published his first Carvalho novel in Spain in 1972. By the time of his death there were more than twenty of them. Carvalho, former member of the Communist Party, ex-CIA agent and loose-living gourmet, is a complex and appealing character. With his one-time convict sidekick Biscuter, he investigates the rottenness at the core of a corrupt and rapidly changing society without ever losing his essential integrity and belief in people.

*Murder in the Central Committee* is not, perhaps the most typical Carvalho novel (not least because the hero spends much time in what are, for him, the deeply uncongenial surroundings of Madrid) but it succeeds brilliantly in blending a clever variant of the classic private eye novel with keen insights into Spain's social and political life. The lights suddenly go out during a meeting of the central committee of the Spanish Communist Party and, when the power is switched back on, the general secretary Fernando Garrido is found murdered. An ex-communist himself, Pepe Carvalho is the obvious choice to investigate the murder and its background of intrigue and corruption. As he looks into the lives of the chief suspects in the case, he is also forced to tread warily through the minefield of Spanish politics and to guard against the deceit and potential betrayals that lurk around every corner.

### ⮒ Read on

*The Angst-Ridden Executive*; *An Olympic Death*

Dominic Martell, *Gitana*; Francisco García Pavón, *The Crimson Twins*; Leonardo Sciascia, *Equal Danger*; Robert Wilson, *A Small Death in Lisbon*

# WALTER MOSLEY (b. 1952) USA

## DEVIL IN A BLUE DRESS (1990)

Mosley's first novel, *Gone Fishin'*, was written in 1988 but rejected by publishers and not until 1990, when *Devil in a Blue Dress* appeared, winning awards, praise and a handy movie rights sale, was his star on the rise. The book introduced a series featuring the good and bad deeds of two black men: Ezekiel 'Easy' Rawlins and his friend, Raymond Alexander, a pint-sized psychopath known as Mouse, as they leave Houston and head for Los Angeles. The books take a cool, considered look at black life in America, from the simple but harsh realities of the 1940s to the complexities and hypocrisies rife in 1950s and '60s LA, a city simmering with racial tension and the pervasive sense of a white supremacy that is unspoken and unchallenged. Finally deemed commercial enough, *Gone Fishin'* eventually appeared in 1997, nearly a decade later, and though Mosley has written several other novels and story collections, all dealing on some level with race, the Easy Rawlins books are probably his best and most successful work.

A sly, skilful revision of *Farewell, My Lovely*, » Raymond Chandler's classic crime novel, *Devil in a Blue Dress* finds Easy in a Negro bar in post-war LA, having been laid off from his job and wondering how he will pay the mortgage on his nice, respectable little home. A white man walks in, flourishing a roll of money, and asking him to help find a white woman, the consort of a notorious gangster. The tough, resourceful but fundamentally decent Easy soon stirs up unrest in South Central's mean streets, uncovering a hotbed of corruption. Aided and abetted by the entertaining, extremely violent Mouse, who represents his darker side, all he has to do is fend off both black and white foes, figure all the angles and stay alive. No wonder he's called Easy.

🎬 **Film version:** *Devil in a Blue Dress* (1995)

🕮 **Read on**

*Black Betty*; *A Little Yellow Dog*; *Always Outnumbered, Always Outgunned* (the first book to feature Socrates Fortlow, a tough and wise ex-con, trying to go straight and finding it a difficult task)
» Chester Himes, *A Rage in Harlem*; Gary Phillips, *Perdition, USA*; James Sallis, *Moth*

## READ ON A THEME: BLACK DETECTIVES

John Ball, *In the Heat of the Night* (Virgil Tibbs)
Grace F. Edwards, *If I Should Die* (Mali Anderson)
Barbara Hambly, *A Free Man of Colour* (Benjamin January)
Gar Anthony Haywood, *Fear of the Dark* (Aaron Gunner)
» Chester Himes, *The Crazy Kill* (Coffin Ed Johnson and Gravedigger Jones)
Hugh Holton, *Violent Crimes* (Larry Cole)
Barbara Neely, *Blanche Cleans Up* (Blanche White)
George Pelecanos, *Right as Rain* (Derek Strange)

# SARA PARETSKY (b. 1947) USA

## INDEMNITY ONLY (1982)

Sara Paretsky attended the universities of her home state of Kansas and also Chicago, the setting of her novels. In 1982, she published the first in a series of books featuring her private investigator, V.I. Warshawski. With Marcia Muller, she spearheaded a new wave of female crime writers that emerged in the 1980s, and proved to be one of the best and one of the most consistent, producing thirteen novels and one story collection. Warshawski, V.I. or Vic for short, differs from the majority of her peers, male and female, in that she is a lawyer *and* a detective, and her work often enters the political arena, a world that is particularly volatile in Chicago, where corruption rears its ugly head. Whilst the books have featured women's issues, such as pro- and anti-abortion stances, there is a strong environmentalist slant too, with urban development and toxic waste coming under Vic's scrutiny. Shrewd, tough and pretty handy with a gun, she is one of the finest characters to have appeared in crime fiction in recent years; the possibility that wedding bells may be heard in the future adds another, highly intriguing twist to her ongoing story.

In *Indemnity Only*, Vic is hired by a man named John Thayer, apparently a prominent banker, to track down a missing woman, Anita Hill, the girlfriend of his son, Peter. What she finds is that neither Thayer nor Anita is who they are supposed to be and that Peter has been killed. No sooner has she made this grisly discovery than Thayer himself vanishes. As she hunts for her erstwhile client to discover who he really is, she becomes dangerously embroiled in a web of deception, fraud and murder. Racing against time, she has to uncover the truth and find the missing girl before the killers do.

### ☙ Read on
*Burn Marks*; *Toxic Shock*; *Tunnel Vision*
Barbara D'Amato, *Hard Women*; **»** Sue Grafton, *E is for Evidence*; Marcia Muller, *Edwin of the Iron Shoes*

# ROBERT B. PARKER (b. 1932) USA

## GOD SAVE THE CHILD (1974)

Spenser, hero of more than a dozen novels by Robert B. Parker, is an updated version of » Chandler's Philip Marlowe, cracking wise and talking tough to disguise the fact that he is a man of sensitivity and intelligence working in a profession where such attributes are not always highly valued. The mean streets he walks are in Boston rather than LA and he is rather more aware of the pressures of political correctness than his predecessor ever was but Spenser is, by some way, the best of those recent private eyes hailed as Marlowe's descendants. In *God Save the Child*, one of the earliest and the best in the series, he is hired by a suburban couple whose teenage son has gone missing. It takes little investigatory skill for him to realize that the Bartletts form an extremely dysfunctional family. The mother is a lush who jumps into bed with any male willing to join her there, the father a weak-willed workaholic who escapes the pressures of home life by immersing himself in his business. Neither has much interest in the children and fifteen-year-old Kevin Bartlett's disappearance seems entirely understandable. But then ransom demands start to turn up at the Bartlett house and a friend and neighbour is found dead in the living room, his neck snapped. Spenser, distracted by his developing relationship with the beautiful Susan Silverman (who becomes a regular in the later books in the series), is forced to deal with a case that is now much more than the search for a teenage runaway.

Robert B. Parker is also the author of two other crime series, one featuring ex-alcoholic cop Jesse Stone, and another a female private eye in Boston named Sunny Randall, but it is the Spenser novels which made his reputation and they remain his greatest achievement.

### ⮂ Read on
*The Judas Goat*; *Looking for Rachel Wallace*; *Night Passage* (the first in a series featuring Jesse Stone); *Poodle Springs* (Parker's creditable attempt to match Chandler by finishing off the manuscript the great man left at his death)
» Raymond Chandler, *The Little Sister*; Arthur Lyons, *Other People's Money*; Lawrence Sanders, *McNally's Luck*

# GEORGE PELECANOS (b. 1957) USA

## A FIRING OFFENCE (1992)
One of the foremost crime writers of recent years, in his dozen novels Pelecanos has gradually sculpted a social history of Washington, DC – the 'dirty city'. Eschewing the world of politics normally associated with this region, he has instead fashioned an alternative portrayal, one that perhaps owes something to the hardboiled novels of the 1950s. Far removed from the well-cut, expense account-lined pockets and sleek limos of Capitol Hill, this DC could also stand for 'disparate communities'. These include poor black neighbourhoods and those peopled by several generations of Greek immigrants. In each of his three series, music plays a big part, setting the period extremely effectively,

whether it is the soul and funk of his 1970s' and '80s' novels like *King Suckerman* and *The Sweet Forever*, the new wave and rock of the Nick Stefanos books or the western movie soundtracks and rap that crop up in the Derek Strange novels. One thing all the books have in common is a powerful, deeply convincing depiction of a harsh universe, one in which losers, victims and a few good people roam, their lives punctuated by such distractions as sex, drugs and alcohol.

The three Nick Stefanos novels were published between 1992 and 1995 and feature the extreme and increasingly dark exploits of Nick, third generation Greek immigrant, reluctant private eye and enthusiastic binge drinker. *A Firing Offence* finds him working at Nutty Nathan's, a hi-fi and electronics store, when one of the young stockboys disappears. His grandfather asks Nick to try to find the boy and, moved by the old man's plea and the fact that the kid reminds him of himself a decade earlier, Nick starts looking. His search uncovers a drug-smuggling ring that's based at Nathan's and, fired for his probing, he soon encounters bloodshed and violence in large proportions.

## ⮧ Read on

*Down by the River Where the Dead Men Go*; *King Suckerman*; *Soul Circus*
» Dennis Lehane, *A Drink Before the War*; Sam Reaves, *A Long Cold Fall*

# ELIZABETH PETERS (b. 1927) USA

## CROCODILE ON THE SANDBANK (1975)

The first of the series of books to feature the late Victorian/Edwardian archaeologist and feminist Amelia Peabody and her husband Radcliffe Emerson, *Crocodile on the Sandbank* provided a blueprint for original and entertaining crime fiction which Elizabeth Peters has followed in nearly twenty other titles. The book and the series opens with spinsterish Amelia, independently wealthy after the death of her scholarly father, travelling to Rome, where she encounters the young Evelyn Barton-Forbes, ruined and abandoned by her callous Latin lover. The two women join forces in a journey to Egypt and, halfway down the Nile, they come across an archaeological dig run by the Emerson brothers – the handsome and charming Walter and the irascible but charismatic Radcliffe. Amelia and Evelyn are both immediately attracted to the life of the archaeologist and they join the brothers in their excavations of the palace of the heretical pharaoh Khuenaten. Amid the developing romance between Evelyn and Walter, and the verbal sparring which Amelia and Radcliffe enjoy, there are mysterious threats to the dig. Workmen refuse to work, servants disappear in the night and, most alarming of all, an ancient mummy seems to have returned to life in order to haunt the archaeologists' camp.

The mysteries in *Crocodile on the Sandbank*, like those which pepper the pages of its sequels, are not the most impenetrable puzzles in all of crime fiction but the strengths of Elizabeth Peters's books lie more in character and dialogue than they do in plotting. The redoubtable Amelia, unflappable and unshakeably self-confident, prepared to confront any danger that Egypt might offer armed only with a sturdy parasol, is one of the most unforgettable creations of contemporary crime fiction. The battle of wits between her and the apparently misogynist Emerson is wonderfully well done and, in later books, their married life and their relationship with their appallingly precocious young son, Ramses, are at the heart of stories that combine charm and excitement in equal measure. Readers starting on the saga of Peabody and Emerson with *Crocodile on the Sandbank* are likely to be inspired to move on to all the others.

## ⮥ Read on

*The Deeds of the Disturber*; *Lion in the Valley*; *The Mummy Case* (three of the best in the Peabody series)
Dorothy Gilman, *The Amazing Mrs Pollifax*; Charlotte MacLeod, *Rest You Merry*; Michael Pearce, *A Cold Touch of Ice*

## READONATHEME: EGYPT (ANCIENT AND OCCASIONALLY MODERN)

» Agatha Christie, *Death Comes as the End*
Paul Doherty, *The Mask of Ra*
Brad Geagley, *Year of the Hyenas*
Anton Gill, *City of the Horizon*
Lauren Haney, *The Right Hand of Amon*
Jessica Mann, *Death Beyond the Nile*
Arthur Phillips, *The Egyptologist*
Lynda S. Robinson, *Murder in the Place of Anubis*

# ELLIS PETERS (1913–95) UK

## ONE CORPSE TOO MANY (1979)

The year is 1138 and England is torn apart by the civil war between the opposing supporters of Stephen and Matilda, rivals for the throne. Shrewsbury is a stronghold for Matilda but Stephen's forces attack the castle there and 94 of Matilda's soldiers die. Brother Cadfael, herbalist and healer in the Benedictine Abbey of Saint Paul and Saint Peter, has the unpleasant duty of preparing the dead for burial but discovers that there is an extra corpse – a victim of a murder that has little to do with the war.

Edith Pargeter wrote dozens of mysteries and historical novels, some under her own name but most using the pseudonym of Ellis Peters. The series of books which feature police officer George Felse and his family is very readable but her greatest creation is the humane and sympathetic medieval monk Brother Cadfael, who uses his knowledge of herbal medicines and his insights into the mysteries of human personality to unravel the crimes that come regularly to trouble the town of Shrewsbury and its monastery. Like so many of the best detective series, Ellis Peters's medieval mysteries depend at least as much on character as they do on plot. Cadfael, whose adventurous past includes a career as a soldier and crusader but who is now content to tend his herb garden, is the focus of the stories but others have their parts to play. *One Corpse Too Many*, for example, introduces the practical man of the world, deputy sheriff Hugh Beringar, whose developing friendship with Cadfael is at the heart of other novels. Some of the later Cadfael stories grow increasingly formulaic and repetitive but in *One*

*Corpse Too Many*, the second in the series, the characters, from Cadfael himself to Beringar, his fellow searcher after truth, are fresh and engaging and mystery and history are neatly combined.

## ⮫ Read on

*A Morbid Taste for Bones*; *Monk's Hood*; *The Virgin in the Ice*; *A Nice Derangement of Epitaphs* (the best of the series featuring Detective Inspector George Felse)
Paul Doherty, *Satan in St Mary's*; Michael Jecks, *The Last Templar*; Kate Sedley, *Death and the Chapman*

## READ ON A THEME: MEDIEVAL MYSTERIES

Alys Clare, *Fortune Like the Moon*
Umberto Eco, *The Name of the Rose*
Alan Gordon, *Thirteenth Night*
Susanna Gregory, *A Plague on Both Your Houses*
Paul Harding, *The Nightingale Gallery*
Bernard Knight, *The Sanctuary Seeker*
A.E. Marston, *The Wolves of Savernake*
Candace Robb, *The Apothecary Rose*
Peter Tremayne, *Absolution by Murder*
Barry Unsworth, *Morality Play*

# EDGAR ALLAN POE (1809–49) USA

## TALES OF MYSTERY AND IMAGINATION

The man largely credited with being the father of the detective story (and who gave his name to the prestigious Edgar Awards), and a pioneer in the science fiction and gothic horror genres, was born in Boston, Massachusetts to travelling actors. At three, he was orphaned, the first of several misfortunes, some clearly self-administered, that plagued his short and often miserable life. He was adopted and, aged seventeen, enrolled at the University of Virginia but his guardian removed him for his gambling debts and general dissipation. Fleeing to Boston, Poe privately published a collection of verse entitled *Tamerlain and Other Poems*. He later sold various poems and stories, all subsequently deemed to be highly influential, as well as finding, and losing, jobs as an editor and reviewer. Living with his aunt in Baltimore, he married her daughter, Virginia, when she was not quite fourteen, and her subsequent death from tuberculosis in 1847 was a heavy blow that doubtless accelerated Poe's own demise two years later, although his excessive drinking was also to blame.

His stories are brilliantly written, poetic and inescapably bleak and morbid. They are peopled by unfortunates hailing from families beset by decay and incest, and individuals whose minds have wandered or collapsed. Invariably, they dwell on such dark topics as torture, necrophilia and murder. Although he wrote around seventy tales, which were of an astonishing range, his reputation in the crime genre rests largely on three works, all featuring the deductive genius of Auguste Dupin. *The Murders in the Rue Morgue* was written in 1841, 46 years before the first

Sherlock Holmes adventure, *The Purloined Letter* appeared in 1845 and *The Mystery of Marie Roget* was published in 1850. Analytical, ingenious and suffused with extensive and often gruesome detail, these stories paved the way for virtually all detective fiction that followed in their wake.

### 🕮 Read on

» Sir Arthur Conan Doyle, *The Adventures of Sherlock Holmes*; Emile Gaboriau, *Monsieur LeCoq*; William Hjortsberg, *Nevermore*; Harold Schechter, *The Mask of Red Death*; Andrew Taylor, *The American Boy*

# IAN RANKIN (b. 1960) UK

## BLACK AND BLUE (1997)

The 'king of tartan *noir*', as one critic has called him, Ian Rankin has written a bestselling series of books featuring his lone-wolf police detective John Rebus. The Rebus novels are set in Edinburgh and portray a city radically different from the traditional tourist image of Princes Street and the Royal Mile. Rankin's Edinburgh is a world of junkie squats, decaying housing estates, gang wars and political corruption. From the very first Rebus novel, *Knots and Crosses*, published in 1987, it was clear that here was a character who was more complex than the run-of-the-mill maverick cop and Rankin has become more and more ambitious as the series has progressed. Later novels do not only reveal the underbelly of tourist Edinburgh; they aim to encompass the whole of

Scottish society and to do so by stretching the boundaries of crime fiction to include territory not usually visited by genre writers.

Probably the best of the entire series is *Black and Blue*, a wonderfully wide-ranging panorama of contemporary Scotland. 'Bible John' was the name given by the media to a serial killer in the 1970s. He was never caught. Now a copycat killer is at work. Rebus, struggling with a drink problem and unsympathetic superiors, has been sidelined. But, as another investigation takes him from Glasgow ganglands to Aberdeen and an offshore oilrig, he is drawn into the web of intrigue and corruption that surrounds the search for the killer now known as 'Johnny Bible'. His own obsession with the earlier case, his loyalty to the memory of an old colleague and his stubborn refusal to acknowledge his need for others come together to threaten Rebus's personal and professional life in a novel that brilliantly combines a sophisticated and complex plot with a convincing exploration of the inner world of its divided and ambiguous central character.

## ⮂ Read on

*Knots and Crosses* (the first Rebus novel); *Let It Bleed*; *Resurrection Men*; *Strip Jack*

Christopher Brookmyre, *Quite Ugly One Morning*; John Harvey, *Still Water*; Bill James, *The Detective is Dead*; Quintin Jardine, *Skinner's Rules*; William McIlvanney, *Laidlaw*

# DEREK RAYMOND (1931–94) UK

## THE DEVIL'S HOME ON LEAVE (1984)

Derek Raymond originally wrote under his real name, Robin Cook and, in the 1960s and 1970s, he produced six novels, mainly about London lowlifes, including *The Crust on Its Uppers* and *A State of Denmark*. After a long hiatus when he lived in France, he returned under the *nom de plume* of Derek Raymond, adopted largely because of the then popularity of a medical thriller writer also named Robin Cook. His new identity brought with it a surge of creativity and he published six novels in his 'Factory' series, so called because of the nickname of the London police station where the unnamed protagonist works. Toiling away in a highly unglamorous division called A14, but also known as the slightly more exotic Department of Unexplained Deaths, he is referred to simply as the Detective Sergeant. Mistrustful of authority, yet sympathetic to those whose lives have become sullied by misfortune, he has a knack for solving the murders of lowly types that no one else can be bothered with, and his investigations often lead to run-ins with the more prestigious detectives in the media-worthy Serious Crimes Division. Dark, grim, often shockingly violent, these are realistic, highly gripping and uniquely powerful British crime novels.

The second of the Factory novels, *The Devil's Home on Leave*, begins with the grisly discovery of a corpse in an abandoned warehouse. The body has been sliced up, boiled and deposited in five bin liners. The nameless policeman soon finds out that this murder is just one incident in a chain of events that the authorities would prefer to be left alone, a situation that only hardens his resolve to solve the case.

Dripping with tension, as the detective and the killer circle one another, this is the best of Raymond's Factory novels.

### ⮂ Read on

*Dead Man Upright*; *He Died With His Eyes Open*; *How the Dead Live*; *I Was Dora Suarez* (all Factory novels)
David Peace, *Nineteen Seventy Four*; Bill Pronzini, *Nightcrawlers*; Mark Timlin, *All the Empty Places*

---

## READONATHEME: BRITISH HARDBOILED

Jake Arnott, *The Long Firm*
Nicholas Blincoe, *Acid Casuals*
Ken Bruen, *London Boulevard*
Jeremy Cameron, *Vinnie Got Blown Away*
Charles Higson, *Full Whack*
Simon Kernick, *The Murder Exchange*
Ted Lewis, *Get Carter* (aka *Jack's Return Home*)
Mark Timlin, *Paint It Black*

---

# RUTH RENDELL (b. 1930) UK

## AN UNKINDNESS OF RAVENS (1985)

One of the most prolific of all British crime novelists, Rendell has produced an enormous number of books of a consistently high quality and originality, helped by the fact that she has three strings to her bow. Her principal offering is the series of novels featuring Chief Inspector Wexford. Finely crafted police procedurals, these are set in the fictional town of Kingsmarkham, a comfortable haven in rural Sussex, and are carried largely by the personality and character of the intelligent and sophisticated Wexford, a humane man often dismayed by the myriad reasons why people are compelled to commit criminal acts. Such reasons and the sort of internal pressures that cause them are also dealt with in the many non-Wexford novels, and, in arguably greater detail, in Rendell's third series of books. These are written under the name of » Barbara Vine and explore a darker, more psychological and often claustrophobic terrain.

*An Unkindness of Ravens* finds Wexford investigating the disappearance of a neighbour, Rodney Williams, in what appears to be a simple, tawdry case of a man leaving his wife and running away with a young woman, but which swiftly becomes something infinitely more sinister. The existence of a militant feminist group, populated by many local girls, and whose symbol is the raven, complicates matters, but Wexford is unprepared for the revelations that follow as he gradually uncovers bigamy, incest and murder. Rendell's excellent characterization, perceptive social observation and faultless plotting make this, possibly, the most memorable of the Wexford novels.

**≋ Read on**

*From Doon With Death*; *Kissing the Gunner's Daughter*; *The Speaker of Mandarin* (all Wexford novels); *Adam and Eve and Pinch Me*; *The Keys to the Street* (non-Wexford)

**»** Colin Dexter, *Last Seen Wearing*; Sheila Radley, *Death and the Maiden*; **»** Peter Robinson, *Cold is the Grave*; Margaret Yorke, *Act of Violence*

# PETER ROBINSON (b. 1950) UK

## IN A DRY SEASON (1999)

Although he has lived in Canada for more than thirty years, Peter Robinson's novels are set in the Yorkshire landscape he remembers from his childhood. The books feature Inspector Alan Banks, a decent and caring man but one often oblivious to the effects of the job on those for whom he cares, and they deftly combine the virtues of old-fashioned English crime fiction with a contemporary concern for the realities of violence, desire and greed. Plots often move smoothly between past and present as they head towards satisfying and convincing resolutions; the supporting cast of characters, from Banks's wife and family to his career-minded superior Chief Constable Jeremiah 'Jimmy' Riddle, have important and ongoing roles to play in the series. The first of the books, *Gallows View*, was published in 1987 and, as the series has progressed, the books have grown more and more ambitious.

*In a Dry Season*, the tenth in the sequence, shows just how skilful a writer Robinson is and why so many fellow crime novelists, from Val McDermid to **»** Michael Connelly, have gone on record as admirers of his work. When drought results in the drying up of a reservoir, the ruins of an old village, submerged decades earlier, resurface. In one of the ruins the skeleton of a woman is found. The woman is a long-dead murder victim and Inspector Banks, languishing in 'career Siberia', is sent to investigate. He and a new colleague, a woman detective sergeant named Cabbot, face the seemingly impossible task of recon-structing a 50-year-old crime. Weaving together an account of Banks's modern investigation and an unpublished crime story which may or may not contain the truth about what happened in the lost village during the Second World War, *In a Dry Season* moves tensely and relentlessly towards the revelation of secrets hidden for many decades.

### ⮂ Read on
*Cold is the Grave*; *Gallows View*; *The Hanging Valley*
Deborah Crombie, *In a Dark House*; **»** Reginald Hill, *On Beulah Height*;
Stuart Pawson, *The Judas Sheep*; Peter Turnbull, *After the Flood*

# DOROTHY L. SAYERS (1893–1957) UK

## THE NINE TAILORS (1934)
At the heart of the world Dorothy L. Sayers created in her books is the urbane and aristocratic Lord Peter Wimsey, one of the greatest of all

amateur detectives to appear in English crime fiction. In many later Wimsey novels much of the attention is focused on his courtship of crime novelist Harriet Vane (they eventually marry and, in *Busman's Honeymoon*, find that crime follows them wherever they go). The pleasures of these novels lie as much in the witty repartee and the unfolding relationship between Wimsey and Vane as they do in the unravelling of the crimes. Other books, in which Wimsey solves the problems without the distraction of a love interest, appeal more strongly to purist fans of crime fiction. Although there are other claimants to the title (*Murder Must Advertise*, for example, is a brilliant portrait of the advertising world in which Sayers herself worked and which she knew very well), *The Nine Tailors* must surely be her most memorable novel. Published after *Strong Poison* introduced Harriet Vane, the book none the less returns to Wimsey on his own, testing his powers of deduction by investigating the mysteries he encounters in the remote East Anglian village of Fenchurch St Paul. The multi-talented Lord Peter steps into the breach when one of the village bell-ringers falls ill on the eve of an ambitious attempt to ring in the New Year with a nine-hour sequence of bells. Some months later, the discovery of an unknown body in a family grave takes him back to Fenchurch St Paul and to an investigation which eventually reveals both how the nameless corpse met its end and what really happened to the Wilbraham Emeralds, stolen many years earlier. Sayers provides one of the most original causes of death in all crime fiction and brilliantly evokes the eerie atmosphere of the fenland landscape in a novel that shows Wimsey at his very best.

🎬 **Film version:** *The Nine Tailors* (TV 1974)

⫘ **Read on**

*Gaudy Night*; *Murder Must Advertise*; *Strong Poison*; *Thrones, Dominations* (an unfinished Wimsey novel that was completed many years after Sayers's death by Jill Paton Walsh)

» Margery Allingham, *Death of a Ghost*; H.C. Bailey, *Shadow on the Wall*; » P.D. James, *Death in Holy Orders*; » Ngaio Marsh, *Off With His Head*

# STEVEN SAYLOR (b. 1956) USA

## ROMAN BLOOD (1991)

There have been many series of mystery novels set in the ancient world but few, if any, have the unmistakable authority of Steven Saylor's books. Other writers provide readers with titbits of historical knowledge grafted on to sometimes creaking plots that could have been set in almost any era; Saylor plunges them into the heart of a sophisticated, cruel and dangerously divided society and provides engrossing stories that could only unfold in that particular world. His descriptions of the sights, smells and sounds of the crowded streets of Rome, the beating heart of what was soon to become a vast empire, carry immediate conviction. His central character, Gordianus the Finder ('the last honest man in Rome', as another character calls him), is a tough, unsentimental but sympathetic hero and we see him ageing and maturing as the series progresses and the perilous politics of the dying days of the

Roman Republic swirl around him, occasionally sweeping him up in conspiracy and murder.

Based on a genuine case involving the Roman orator and politician Cicero, the first in the Gordianus series showed immediately Saylor's talent for blending real history with fictional mystery. Events described by Latin historians are recreated and re-imagined as real individuals share the pages with characters of Saylor's own invention. In *Roman Blood*, the up-and-coming Cicero hires Gordianus to investigate the background to a murder case in which he is defending a man charged with killing his father. The crime seems at first to be a personal one, involving family hatreds and material greed, but, as he digs deeper, Gordianus finds that the case goes to the very heart of the political corruption and infighting in the Roman Republic. The personal and the political are inextricably intertwined, as they have proved to be in all the absorbing novels which have followed Saylor's outstanding debut.

## 🕮 Read on

*Last Seen in Massilia*; *A Murder on the Appian Way*; *A Twist at the End* (Saylor's non-series novel, set in late nineteenth-century Texas)

Lindsey Davis, *The Silver Pigs* (the first volume in Davis's series featuring the Roman investigator Marcus Didius Falco); David Wishart, *White Murder*

## READ ON A THEME: MURDER IN THE ANCIENT WORLD

Anna Apostolou, *A Murder in Macedon*
Ron Burns, *Roman Nights*
Margaret Doody, *Aristotle Detective*
Michael Edwards, *Murder at the Panionic Games*
Jane Finnis, *A Bitter Chill*
Albert Noyer, *The Cybeline Conspiracy*
John Maddox Roberts, *SPQR: The King's Gambit*
Rosemary Rowe, *The Germanicus Mosaic*
José Carlos Somoza, *The Athenian Murders*
Marilyn Todd, *I, Claudia*

# GEORGES SIMENON (1903–89) Belgium

## MAIGRET SETS A TRAP (1965)

Georges Joseph Christian Simenon was born in Liège and, after becoming a journalist on the *Gazette de Liège* in 1919, moved to Paris in 1922. Here, he started writing fiction, continuing until the 1970s, by which time he had produced hundreds of novels. As impressive as his astonishing prolificacy was his consistency, since his output was of an extremely high standard, and his 350 or so psychological novels, teeming with characters who were driven, desperate, and sometimes deranged, were particularly lauded. Foremost of his prodigious efforts was his creation of the tenacious, pipe-smoking Commissaire Jules Maigret of the Paris police. The first novel featuring this imperturbable sleuth, *The Death of Monsieur Gallet*, appeared in 1931, and was followed by around a hundred more. Each one is short, written in a spare, streamlined style, and coloured by vivid, atmospheric descriptions of the smoke-filled bars and modest apartments lying tucked away in streets splashed by downpours of murky rain. The avuncular Maigret's chatty but relentless questioning of people is one of the prominent highlights in a series blessed with a great many.

In *Maigret Sets a Trap*, the Commissaire's formidable coolness, logic and powers of deduction are stretched to the limit when five women are stabbed to death in Montmartre, and the killer remains at large. Working feverishly in a scorching summer heatwave, Maigret is stymied, his frustration and anger mounting daily. In a bid to apprehend the killer by appealing to his own grisly vanity, Maigret decides to set a trap, but is wracked with guilt when it results in another death. When he finally succeeds in discovering three suspects, he finds they are so tightly ensnared in a web of guilt and obsession that it takes all of his powers to dismantle it and uncover the twisted motive behind the murders.

## ⮑ Read on

*Maigret and the Burglar's Wife*; *My Friend Maigret*; *Maigret Travels South*; *Maigret and the Reluctant Witnesses* (Maigret novels); *The Man Who Watched the Trains Go By*; *The Stain on the Snow* (non-Maigret novels)

Nicolas Freeling, *King of the Rainy Country*; Graham Greene, *A Gun for Sale*; Sebastien Japrisot, *The Lady in a Car With Glasses and a Gun*

# MICKEY SPILLANE (1918–2006) USA

## KISS ME, DEADLY (1952)

Mickey Spillane was a pugnacious writer, knocking out novels as fast as his private eye and alleged alter ego, Mike Hammer, knocked out the bad guys and girls, and he remains a legendary, perhaps notorious, figure in crime fiction. Hammer burst on to the scene in 1947, stuck fast in the Cold War, a period of paranoia, bigotry and mob hatred that suited him fine and from which he never really emerged. The first multi-million-selling cycle of Hammer novels ended in 1952, after which Spillane stopped writing and joined the Jehovah's Witnesses, a conversion that may explain the Old Testament-style titles gracing some of his books, such as *I, the Jury* and *Vengeance is Mine*.

Stylistically bereft, though radiating a cheap, potent excitement, the Hammer books are either loved or loathed, depending on the reader's attitude towards violence, sexism and casual racism. Seemingly indestructible, Hammer slugs it out with mobsters, communists, treacherous women and anyone who gets in his way. To call his methods crude is an understatement of epic proportions. Compared with Hammer, Sam Spade and Philip Marlowe are as cerebral and sedentary as Mycroft Holmes.

*Kiss Me, Deadly* was the sixth in the series and was soon made into a surprisingly good *noir* movie. Hammer swears to avenge the murder of a woman whom he gallantly picked up when she threw herself in front of his car, and his thirst for vengeance leads him to the Mafia and the hunt for a case and its mysterious contents. Everybody is desperate to get their hands on it, and it is down to the redoubtable Hammer to grab it first. Plot and characterization fly out of the window as fast as bullets and in their place come lashings of deliriously depicted violence, prurient sex and a shattering conclusion.

🎬 **Film version:** *Kiss Me Deadly* (1955)

📖 **Read on**

*I, the Jury*; *My Gun is Quick*; *Vengeance is Mine*

Michael Avallone, *Lust is No Lady*; Peter Cheyney, *Your Deal, My Lovely*; Max Allan Collins, *Two for the Money*; Carroll John Daly, *The Adventures of Race Williams*; Richard S. Prather, *Have Gat – Will Travel*

# RICHARD STARK (b. 1933) USA

## THE HUNTER (aka POINT BLANK) (1962)

Richard Stark is one of the two pseudonyms used by Donald E. Westlake, a prolific, highly skilled crime novelist, who, under his own name, has written tough thrillers and humorous 'caper' novels, notably the Burglar series, featuring John Dortmunder, an amiable, generally ineffective thief. Under his other pseudonym of Tucker Coe, Westlake has written five novels featuring Mitch Tobin, a former policeman, drummed out of the force for corruption and for inadvertently causing his partner's death, for which he remains racked with guilt. Despite his mistakes, Tobin is tough, resourceful and silent, and is a somewhat lighter, more human version of Parker, the character that Westlake created as Richard Stark. A thief and killer, Parker is a career criminal with no morals, no fear and no time to waste on nonsense like emotions or warmth; a stoical, implacable figure whose sense of purpose, cold logic and tunnel vision make him a cross between a Zen master and a robot. If someone is in his way, they won't be for long. Stark's most memorable achievement is to convince the reader that, against their better judgement, they want Parker to succeed, turning him into the most extreme of anti-heroes, but still a hero, nevertheless.

Parker first appeared in 1962 in *The Hunter*, later filmed as *Point Blank*, starring the excellently-cast Lee Marvin. Betrayed, shot and left for dead in a burning house by his wife and former partner after a successful score, Parker is now out for revenge. He wants to get his hands on his wife, on Mal, his double-crossing partner and on his share of the money. If Mal has used his money to square things with the Mob, then Parker will have to tackle them too. Hugely effective and addictive, a seemingly impossible combination of power and restraint, this is, like Parker himself, impossible to resist.

📖 **Film version:** *Point Blank* (1967); *Payback* (1999)

🐍 **Read on**

As Stark: *The Black Ice Score*; *Deadly Edge*; *The Man With the Getaway Face*; *The Outfit*; *The Rare Coin Score*; *Slayground* (all Parker novels)

As Coe: *Don't Lie to Me*; *Kinds of Love, Kinds of Death*; *Murder Among Children*; *Wax Apple* (all Mitch Tobin novels)

As Donald E. Westlake: *Don't Ask*; *The Hot Rock*; *Nobody's Perfect* (all John Dortmunder novels)

# REX STOUT (1886–1975) USA

## THE LEAGUE OF FRIGHTENED MEN (1935)

Few protagonists in crime fiction are as memorable as the mountainous gourmet and orchid-fancier Nero Wolfe, who appeared in more than forty novels by Rex Stout from the 1930s to the 1970s. Too slothful to leave the confines of his luxurious apartment, Wolfe makes use of the photographic memory and resourcefulness of his assistant and leg-man Archie Goodwin to gather the information he needs to solve the bizarre problems clients bring him. In *The League of Frightened Men*, which Stout regularly claimed was his own favourite among his books, Wolfe is approached by a group of men who were all classmates at Harvard 25 years earlier. Through all this time the men have been haunted by an undergraduate prank that went horribly wrong, leaving a student named Paul Chapin permanently crippled. Plagued by guilt, they have supported Chapin financially during his later career as a writer but now he appears to be contemplating a belated vengeance. A reunion party ended in the death of one of the classmates and now others are receiving anonymous letters and poems threatening them with similar retribution. It is up to Nero Wolfe, with the help of Archie Goodwin, to unearth the truth and unmask a very devious murderer.

The genius of Rex Stout was that he saw a way to combine two very different styles of crime fiction in one series. Nero Wolfe, with his unusual tastes, hobbies and appearance, is a classic example of the detective as eccentric amateur found particularly in English crime novels of the Golden Age. Archie Goodwin, pounding the city streets in search of the evidence Wolfe needs to perform his feats of deduction, owes something to the then newly developing style of hardboiled American fiction. Together they form one of the most entertaining and lively partnerships in the history of crime fiction and *The League of Frightened Men*, their second outing in print, remains one of the best examples of the duo at work.

🎬 **Film version:** *The League of Frightened Men* (1937)

📖 **Read on**
*Black Orchids*; *Fer-de-Lance*; *Some Buried Caesar*
Anthony Boucher, *The Case of the Crumpled Knave*; Ellery Queen, *The Greek Coffin Mystery*; S.S. Van Dine, *The Canary Murder Case*

# JULIAN SYMONS (1912–94) UK

## A THREE PIPE PROBLEM (1975)

As well as being a distinguished crime author and anthologist, Julian Symons was an extraordinarily versatile and productive writer who, in the course of a 50-year career, published books on subjects as diverse as General Gordon and the siege of Khartoum and the General Strike. In his novels of the 1950s and '60s, he added a psychological depth to traditional English crime fiction which it had rarely shown before. *The Colour of Murder*, for example, which was first published in 1957, is a study of a man who is charged with the murder of a young woman with whom he has become obsessed. None the less, these psychological crime stories now seem rather dated and rooted in the period in which they were written. Perhaps more rewarding for a modern reader are the two witty and erudite pastiches Symons wrote in which a small-time thespian named Sheridan Haynes, who idolizes Sherlock Holmes, gets opportunities to emulate his hero. The first of these is *A Three Pipe Problem*, in which Haynes, delighted by his chance to play Holmes in a TV series, becomes convinced that he can apply his talents off screen as well as on and solve the mystery behind the so-called Karate Killings, murders committed by a single chop to the neck. The book deftly mixes a genuinely puzzling crime story, complete with clues and red herrings scattered through the text, with all the fun that can be extracted from the Holmesian allusions and parallels. Symons returned to the character of Sheridan Haynes in *The Kentish Manor Mysteries*, a convoluted story involving murder, a wealthy Holmesian collector and a lost Conan Doyle manuscript. This is also an enjoyable read but *A Three Pipe Problem* is not only better but one of the finest of the many books Symons published in his long career.

## ⮂ **Read on**

*The Colour of Murder*; *The Man Who Killed Himself*
Simon Brett, *Cast, in Order of Disappearance*; **»** Ngaio Marsh, *Night at the Vulcan*

# JOSEPHINE TEY (1896/97–1952) UK

## THE FRANCHISE AFFAIR (1948)

Robert Blair, a country solicitor, is asked to represent Marion Sharpe and her elderly mother, who are accused of kidnapping, beating and imprisoning a young girl. The girl, Betty Kane, unerringly identifies the women and their house and Blair takes on the seemingly impossible task of showing that she is lying. An updated version of a real-life *cause célèbre* of the eighteenth century, *The Franchise Affair*, one of the few classic crime novels in which the crime is not murder, is a penetrating and subtle study of apparently motiveless malignancy. Why has Betty Kane chosen to direct such accusations against seemingly blameless women? And are Marion Sharpe and her mother really as innocent as Blair believes them to be? *The Franchise Affair* is a novel rooted in the era in which it is set – the details of cramped and confined life in a small town of the period are brilliantly recreated – but its examination of spite and envy and the disturbing power of gossip to destroy lives still rings true.

Josephine Tey was one of the pseudonyms of the Scottish writer Elizabeth Mackintosh (she also wrote plays, successful in their day, under the name Gordon Daviot) and the detective novels she wrote, mostly in the last ten years of her life, have long been acclaimed as classics of the genre. The best known of her books is *The Daughter of Time*, in which her series character Inspector Grant, convalescing in hospital after breaking his leg, is intrigued by a mysterious portrait which turns out to be that of Richard III, supposedly responsible for the murder of the Princes in the Tower. Unconvinced that the face is that of a ruthless killer, Grant begins a bedridden investigation into a centuries-old crime. The result is a mystery novel, like *The Franchise Affair*, of remarkable originality.

🍴 **Film versions:** *The Franchise Affair* (1950); *The Franchise Affair* (TV 1988)

📖 **Read on**
*The Daughter of Time*; *The Singing Sands*
» Colin Dexter, *The Wench is Dead* (like Tey's *The Daughter of Time*, a story in which the central protagonist investigates a crime from the past)

# ROSS THOMAS (1926–95) USA

## THE FOOLS IN TOWN ARE ON OUR SIDE (1970)

A wonderful thriller writer and crime novelist, Thomas's career spanned nearly three decades, beginning in 1965 with his first novel, *The Cold War Swap*, which garnered an Edgar Award for Best First Mystery. He wrote 24 others, all well received and winning increasing praise. A professional life spent going from one job to another, often with a political bent, such as campaign manager, union spokesman and foreign correspondent, gave him a taste for intrigue and deal-making, something he captured perfectly in his fiction. The novels feature lots of behind-the-scenes action, handled by characters – women as well as men – who are movers and shakers, yet remain shadowy figures, turning their anonymity into a form of strength. Political power and concomitant sums of money change hands, while careers are made and destroyed. In hotel rooms, offices and corporate boardrooms, shrewd, smart, cynical individuals do battle with their wits and other, less subtle, weapons. They know the score, how to play the game, how to cut a deal and when to cut and run and Thomas portrays them all brilliantly.

With its title smoothly borrowed from Mark Twain's classic, *Huckleberry Finn*, Thomas's sixth novel, *The Fools in Town Are on Our Side*, is the riveting tale of Lucifer Dye. Dye is a slick operator who has recently been dismissed from Section Two, a clandestine American intelligence agency. Approached by a man named Victor Orcutt, the unemployed Dye is offered a job. What Orcutt does is to clean up tainted, disreputable cities, but he improves them by first making them worse. So all Dye has to do is to corrupt a whole city, just a small one, on the Gulf Coast. Tautly plotted, brimming with deception and full of crackling dialogue, this is classic Thomas, which makes it very good indeed.

## ⮂ **Read on**

*Briarpatch*; *Cast a Yellow Shadow*; *Missionary Stew*; *Voodoo, Ltd*
» Lawrence Block, *The Thief Who Couldn't Sleep*; John R. Maxim, *The Bannerman Solution*

# JIM THOMPSON (1906–77) USA

## THE KILLER INSIDE ME (1952)

Lou Ford is the deputy sheriff of a small Texas town. Outwardly a respected and well-liked member of the community, he carries a dark secret from his past and the sickness that overwhelmed him once before is about to return. Jim Thompson was a writer largely ignored by the critics during his lifetime but, since his death, his reputation as a master of *noir* fiction has grown and grown. In *The Killer Inside Me*, he shows just how successfully he could take a standard 'pulp' tale and invest it with his own originality and style. Using a first person narrative, which brilliantly captures both Lou Ford's inner voice and his ability to project an image of untroubled normality, Thompson transcends the limitations of his story to create a chilling portrait of a warped psyche lurking beneath an apparently ordinary surface.

In more than twenty novels, most of them first published, in lurid and garishly coloured covers, as cheap paperback originals in the 1940s and 1950s, Thompson pursued a vision of a small-town America peopled by grifters, corrupt cops, brooding drunks and psychopathic loners which is unsettling but grimly compelling. In the world he created there is little morality and few constraints. Individuals pursue their own aims and desires with little concern for others, blundering through life in search of some kind of redemption as fate leads them in a bitter dance towards death. The suspense in Thompson's novels – and there is plenty of it – comes not from observing the unravelling of any mysteries in the plot but from watching his characters twisting and turning in their desperate attempts to escape that fate. Thompson was an unrepentant pessimist about human beings and *The Killer Inside Me* embodies his cruel vision of a dog-eat-dog society more memorably than any other of his novels.

🎬 **Film version:** *The Killer Inside Me* (1976)

📖 **Read on**
*The Grifters*; *A Hell of a Woman*; *Pop. 1280*; *Wild Town*
» James M. Cain, *The Postman Always Rings Twice*; » David Goodis, *Dark Passage*

# BARBARA VINE (b. 1930) UK

## A FATAL INVERSION (1987)
Under the pseudonym of Barbara Vine, » Ruth Rendell has written a series of psychological thrillers which are distinguished by the subtlety with which they draw readers into tangled webs of love, guilt and remorse. They deftly probe the complex, volatile relationships that exist among families and friends, or between members of small communities, they are simply but highly effectively told and, in their quiet power and ability to resonate disturbingly in the reader's mind, share something with the work of » Patricia Highsmith. Often their plots revolve around the slow revelation of secrets from the past or the gradual emergence of the truth about an individual's history and character from the lies and deceit in which he or she has sought to cloak them.

In *A Fatal Inversion*, the first book published under the pseudonym, all the qualities which have made the Barbara Vine novels so powerful, were already in place. A couple who have recently moved into a Suffolk country house unearth bones in the pets' cemetery kept by earlier owners which belong to no dog or cat or guinea pig. The skeletons they find are those of a young woman and a very young baby. When news of the discovery hits the morning papers, there are several people who stir uneasily in their chairs at breakfast. Ten years earlier, in 1976, Adam Verne-Smith was a young student who had unexpectedly inherited the country house from a great-uncle. Together with a close friend, a medical student named Rufus Fletcher, and a small group of waifs and strays they had picked up, Adam had spent the long, hot summer that year living in the house. An apparent idyll of sunbathing, sex and wine-bibbing had turned into a catastrophe which all present had long believed was forgotten. The discovery of the bodies threatens to bring it all to light. The skill with which Rendell/Vine marshals her plot is remarkable. Readers know that something terrible happened in that summer of 1976 but, as details are gradually and tantalizingly revealed bit by bit and the truth is slowly approached, the tension in the narrative builds to almost unbearable levels. The ironic conclusion, that manages to be both long-expected and utterly surprising at the same time, is a fitting ending to a magnificently suspenseful novel.

## ≋ Read on

*Asta's Book*; *The Chimney Sweeper's Boy*; *Gallowglass*
Frances Fyfield, *The Nature of the Beast*; » Minette Walters, *The Sculptress*

# MINETTE WALTERS (b. 1949) UK

## THE ICE HOUSE (1992)

An unidentified and decomposing body is found in the ice house in the grounds of Streech Grange, the home of Phoebe Maybury and her two companions, Anne Cattrell and Diana Goode. To the police, arriving to investigate, the answer is clear. The body must be that of Phoebe's husband who disappeared ten years earlier. One of the officers was involved in the search for the husband at the time and he is in no doubt that Phoebe escaped justice at the time. To the neighbours the discovery is merely confirmation of their prejudiced suspicions about the unconventional *ménage à trois* in which the women have lived. As Walters's cunningly contrived plot unfolds, hidden passions and carefully concealed secrets begin to emerge. The police obsession with pinning responsibility for the murder on the three women obscures the real identity of the corpse and the truth behind the death.

Like so many of the best contemporary writers of crime fiction, Minette Walters produces books which are not so much 'whodunits' in the old-fashioned sense but 'whydunits'. The emphasis is not just upon the twists and turns of a puzzling plot but upon the way in which the narrative slowly reveals more and more about the hidden psychology of her characters. *The Ice House* was her debut novel and she has followed it with a succession of other stories which combine strong plots and complex characters. From *The Sculptress*, a tale of a woman imprisoned for family murders she may or may not have committed, to *The Shape of Snakes*, the story of a teacher's twenty-year obsession with proving that the death of a psychologically damaged woman was murder, Walters's books return again and again to similar themes but they do so with an invention and an ingenuity that makes all of them worth reading.

### ⮒ Read on
*The Sculptress*; *The Scold's Bridle*
Jane Adams, *The Greenway*; Nicci French, *Beneath the Skin*; Andrew Taylor, *The Barred Window*; **»** Barbara Vine, *The Chimney Sweeper's Boy*

## JOSEPH WAMBAUGH (b. 1937) USA

### THE CHOIRBOYS (1975)
Few are better equipped to write about the legendary Los Angeles Police Department than Joseph Wambaugh, the son of a Pittsburgh police officer, who served with the LAPD for fourteen years. He had been with them for over a decade when he published his first novel, *The New Centurions*, in 1971. His first non-fiction book, *The Onion Field*, appeared in 1974 and was hugely successful, winning him the first of two Edgar Awards. Having retired from the force, Wambaugh became a full-time writer, producing several highly successful novels, most of them adorned with a powerful and extremely dark humour, often employed as a counterpoint to the accounts of various crimes.

Although the setting of the sun-kissed southern California landscape is a crowded field, Wambaugh's depiction of the corruption and moral decay rampant in this idyllic haven deserves special mention. With their marked absence of media-savvy top brass, distinguished district attorneys and wisecracking detectives, the novels present a convincing portrayal of hard-working police officers. In the melting pot that is LA, with its black, white, Asian and Hispanic legions, the only colour that matters is the blue-black hue of the uniform, a detail that's paramount in all of Wambaugh's books.

Often cited as his finest novel and filmed in 1977, *The Choirboys* was written after its author had read and been influenced by Joseph Heller's *Catch-22*. Published after Wambaugh had left the force, it begins with a simple statement about a killing in MacArthur Park. Offering a tautly written story of ten regular, hard-working cops, who meet in the park when they are off duty for 'choir practice', a stress-relieving pastime that includes swapping stories, drinking and indulging in acts of violence, Wambaugh tells each cop's tale, masterfully drawing in the reader as he gradually reveals the details that lead back to the killing.

🎬 **Film version:** *The Choirboys* (1977)

📖 **Read on**
*The Delta Star*; *The New Centurions*
William Caunitz, *One Police Plaza*; Gerald Petievich, *To Live and Die in LA*

# CHARLES WILLEFORD (1919–88) USA

## MIAMI BLUES (1984)

Before he became a novelist, Charles Willeford was a soldier. He enlisted at the age of sixteen in 1935, during the Depression, and served in the Army Air Corps, a term during which he was stationed mainly in Manila, in the Philippines, and later in the Cavalry. His hair-raising, dissolute and often fairly seedy experiences formed the basis for an autobiography, *Something About a Soldier*, published in 1986. After being discharged in 1938, he went to Los Angeles, but following some trouble in the city's Skid Row area, decided to re-enlist. In the 1950s and '60s, he began writing hardboiled novels, all published by paperback houses, but with little real success. Although these early books have been compared with the novels of » Jim Thompson, the two writers have little in common, other than a vaguely 'pulp' background, and a more appropriate comparison might be Charles Bukowski. Real acclaim and commercial success came in the 1980s, when Willeford wrote his series of four crime novels, set in Florida and featuring the downbeat, disgruntled cop, Detective Hoke Moseley.

The first of these, *Miami Blues*, was made into a well-received film and saw Willeford shrugging off his pulp leanings and enter Elmore Leonard-esque territory, as he introduced, with more of a shrug than a flourish, the amiable if generally unprepossessing Moseley, a less-than-glamorous policeman with money problems, a tendency towards depression and false teeth. After a gruelling day spent investigating a quadruple homicide, Hoke just wants to unwind but, when psychopath Freddy Frenger Jr, with a dozy hooker in tow, knocks him out and steals his gun, badge and dentures, then his day gets a lot worse. Hilarious, tough and utterly convincing in its portrayal of the criminally deranged Freddy and the dishevelled but dogged Hoke, this is probably Willeford's finest novel.

**Film version:** *Miami Blues* (1990)

## Read on

*New Hope for the Dead*; *Sideswipe*; *The Way We Die Now* (the other three Hoke Moseley novels); *The Burnt Orange Heresy*
» James W. Hall, *Blackwater Sound*; » Jim Thompson, *The Getaway*

---

### READONATHEME: FLORIDA CRIMES

Edna Buchanan, *Miami, It's Murder*
Tim Dorsey, *Orange Crush*
Carolina Garcia-Aguilera, *Bitter Sugar*
» Carl Hiaasen, *Double Whammy*
» Stuart M. Kaminsky, *Vengeance*
» Elmore Leonard, *Stick*
John Lutz, *Tropical Heat*
» Ed McBain, *Goldilocks*
Lawrence Sanders, *McNally's Secret*
Laurence Shames, *Florida Straits*
Randy Wayne White, *Tampa Burn*

---

# CHARLES WILLIAMS (1909–75) USA

## DEAD CALM (1963)

Williams was born in Texas and lived there and in New Mexico, where he worked as a merchant marine before joining the navy during the war. The sea and sailing played a large part in his life and appeared in several of his 22 novels. He is a writer who, despite considerable success with his books and subsequent film adaptations, is now criminally neglected. His first novel, the mildly salacious *Hill Girl*, was published by famous paperback house Gold Medal in 1950, selling more than 1,200,000 copies, and was followed, unsurprisingly, by *Big City Girl* and *River Girl*. Several of his novels were filmed, and sometimes scripted by Williams himself, and many of them, if not set at sea, such as *Dead Calm*, were in small towns, usually overheated, humid places on the Gulf Coast and south Florida. Some were extremely funny, but the majority featured either sympathetic characters who courageously prevail when caught up in evil situations, or opportunistic, sneaky types lured by duplicitous beauties and the promise of riches. Williams wrote brilliantly and consistently for over two decades, but after the death of his wife in the early 1970s and the waning popularity of his kind of fiction, he committed suicide in 1975.

*Dead Calm* begins peacefully, with honeymoon couple John and Rae Ingram alone on their yacht in the Pacific Ocean, when they see on the horizon a ship sinking slowly. They rescue the ship's remaining passenger, who claims that the others on board have died from food poisoning. Ingram is suspicious and rows over to see for himself, before realizing that he is marooned on a death ship, leaving his wife in the hands of a deadly lunatic. The lyrical descriptions of aquatic tranquillity only serve to highlight the suspense and tension of this tautly written, perfectly titled book.

🎬 **Film version:** *Dead Calm* (1989)

🐚 **Read on**
*Aground*; *The Diamond Bikini*; *Hell Hath No Fury* (aka *The Hot Spot*); *Sailcloth Shroud*; *Scorpion Reef*; *A Touch of Death*
» Jim Thompson, *Savage Night*; W.L. Heath, *Violent Saturday*

# DANIEL WOODRELL (b. 1953) USA

## UNDER THE BRIGHT LIGHTS (1986)

Born and bred in the Ozark Mountains, where he continues to live, Woodrell is the master of what he himself has described as 'Country Noir', tales of white trash feuding and petty criminality in the backwoods of the Southern states. Although the characters in them are nearly all on the wrong side of the law and violence simmers continually beneath the surface of their lives, Woodrell's most recent novels (*Tomato Red, The Death of Sweet Mister, Winter's Bone*) are not really crime novels. There are few mysteries and puzzles in them beyond the permanent ones of human motivation and personality. However, his three early novels, set in the imaginary Louisiana city of

St Bruno, are more conventional examples of crime fiction.

In *Under the Bright Lights*, a black councilman who has been rocking the boat of local politics is found shot dead after what seems like a failed burglary. The burglar, people assume, must be the killer. Detective René Shade is not convinced and his search for the real truth leads him into the violence of the Cajun and black quarters of St Bruno and into the corruption and chicanery surrounding its city hall. Hindered rather than helped by the involvement of his two brothers, Tip, a bar-owner with a finger in too many possibly illegal pies, and assistant district attorney François, Shade has to negotiate his way through dangerous waters. Woodrell's debut novel shows all his strengths as a writer already in place. Dialogue is sharp and pungently witty; descriptive prose has an offbeat originality which demands attention. Characters, from the Shade brothers to the cocky, dim-witted country boy, Jewel Cobb, who is sent to the city as an assassin, are brought immediately to life. Woodrell has since moved on from St Bruno but it is a city crime fiction readers will still enjoy visiting.

## ⮂ Read on

*The Death of Sweet Mister*; *The Ones You Do*; *Tomato Red*
» James Lee Burke, *Jolie Blon's Bounce*; Christopher Cook, *Robbers*

# CORNELL WOOLRICH (1903–68) USA

## THE BRIDE WORE BLACK (1940)

Widely known as a master of suspense, Woolrich was a prolific pulp writer who wrote under different pseudonyms, turning out hundreds of stories and 25 novels by the time of his death. An introvert, repressed homosexual and heavy drinker, for most of his adult life he lived in hotels with his mother, on whom he was fixated and whose death in 1957 marked the beginning of his decline. For three decades, he was extremely successful, his stories published in magazines and adapted for cinema, radio and television, the most famous being Alfred Hitchcock's film of *Rear Window*, while his novels sold well and many were also filmed. But he was cursed by an overwhelming sense of doom, feeling like an 'insect' that was trapped 'inside a downturned glass' and most of his characters were similarly ensnared. When he died he was diabetic, alcoholic and had had his leg amputated due to gangrene. He had virtually stopped writing, but royalties continued to pour in, and his estate was valued at nearly a million dollars.

*The Bride Wore Black* inaugurated the famous Black Series, which consisted of six novels and ended in 1948 with *Rendezvous in Black*. It is the unbearably painful story of a bride, Julie Killen, whose husband is killed on their wedding day, on the steps of the church just moments after they were married, by five drunk drivers in a speeding car. She vows to avenge her husband's death and sets out to find each of the men, spending years tracking them down and, one by one, killing them. But policeman Lew Wanger knows something else about her husband's death and is on her trail, desperately trying to stop her before she honours her deadly vow. Dark, tautly written and feverishly plotted, this is prime Woolrich.

🎬 **Film version:** *The Bride Wore Black* (1967)

🐚 **Read on**

*Black Alibi*; *The Black Angel*; *The Black Curtain*; *The Black Path of Fear*; *Rendezvous in Black*

» Lawrence Block, *Mona*; » Fredric Brown, *The Screaming Mimi*; Steve Fisher, *I Wake Up Screaming*; » David Goodis, *The Blonde on the Street Corner*

# CRIMEFICTIONAWARDS

## EDGAR AWARD

Named in honour of Edgar Allan Poe, the Edgar Awards are awarded by the Mystery Writers of America and are the most prestigious crime writing awards in the USA. There are awards in several categories but it is the award for the Best Mystery of the Year that is the most important. This is the list of those authors and books which have won Best Mystery of the Year since the award was inaugurated in 1954.

| 1954 | Charlotte Jay *Beat Not the Bones* |
| 1955 | » Raymond Chandler *The Long Goodbye* |
| 1956 | » Margaret Millar *Beast in View* |
| 1957 | Charlotte Armstrong *A Dram of Poison* |
| 1958 | Ed Lacy *Room to Swing* |
| 1959 | Stanley Ellin *The Eighth Circle* |
| 1960 | Celia Fremlin *The Hours Before Darkness* |
| 1961 | » Julian Symons *Progress of a Crime* |
| 1962 | J.J. Marric *Gideon's Fire* |
| 1963 | » Ellis Peters *Death of the Joyful Woman* |
| 1964 | » Eric Ambler *The Light of Day* |
| 1965 | John Le Carré *The Spy Who Came in from the Cold* |

| 1966 | Adam Hall *The Quiller Memorandum* |
| 1967 | Nicolas Freeling *King of the Rainy Country* |
| 1968 | Donald E. Westlake *God Save the Mark* |
| 1969 | Jeffrey Hudson *A Case of Need* |
| 1970 | » Dick Francis *Forfeit* |
| 1971 | Maj Sjowall and Per Wahloo *The Laughing Policeman* |
| 1972 | Frederick Forsyth *The Day of the Jackal* |
| 1973 | Warren Kiefer *The Lingala Code* |
| 1974 | » Tony Hillerman *Dance Hall of the Dead* |
| 1975 | Jon Cleary *Peter's Pence* |
| 1976 | Brian Garfield *Hopscotch* |
| 1977 | » Robert B. Parker *Promised Land* |
| 1978 | William Hallahan *Catch Me, Kill Me* |
| 1979 | Ken Follett *The Eye of the Needle* |
| 1980 | Arthur Maling *The Rheingold Route* |
| 1981 | » Dick Francis *Whip Hand* |
| 1982 | William Bayer *Peregrine* |
| 1983 | Rick Boyer *Billingsgate Shoal* |
| 1984 | » Elmore Leonard *La Brava* |
| 1985 | » Ross Thomas *Briarpatch* |
| 1986 | L.R. Wright *The Suspect* |
| 1987 | » Barbara Vine *A Dark-Adapted Eye* |
| 1988 | Aaron Elkins *Old Bones* |
| 1989 | » Stuart M. Kaminsky *A Cold Red Sunrise* |
| 1990 | » James Lee Burke *Black Cherry Blues* |
| 1991 | Julie Smith *New Orleans Mourning* |
| 1992 | » Lawrence Block *A Dance at the Slaughterhouse* |

1993    Margaret Maron *Bootlegger's Daughter*

1994    » Minette Walters *The Sculptress*

1995    Mary Willis Walker *The Red Scream*

1996    » Dick Francis *Come to Grief*

1997    Thomas H. Cook *The Chatham School Affair*

1998    » James Lee Burke *Cimarron Rose*

1999    Robert Clark *Mr. White's Confession*

2000    Jan Burke *Bones*

2001    » Joe R. Lansdale *The Bottoms*

2002    T. Jefferson Parker *Silent Joe*

2003    S.J. Rozan *Winter and Night*

2004    » Ian Rankin *Resurrection Men*

2005    T. Jefferson Parker *California Girl*

## THE CWA GOLD DAGGER

Originally named the Crossed Red Herrings Award, this award, presented by the Crime Writers' Association, was renamed the Golden Dagger in 1960.

1955    Winston Graham *The Little Walls*

1956    Edward Grierson *The Second Man*

1957    » Julian Symons *The Colour of Murder*

1958    Margot Bennett *Someone From the Past*

1959    » Eric Ambler *Passage of Arms*

1960    Lionel Davidson *The Night of Wenceslas*

1961    Mary Kelly *The Spoilt Kill*

1962    Joan Fleming *When I Grow Rich*

| 1963 | John Le Carré *The Spy Who Came in From the Cold* |
| 1964 | H.R.F. Keating *The Perfect Murder* |
| 1965 | » Ross Macdonald *The Far Side of the Dollar* |
| 1966 | Lionel Davidson *A Long Way to Shiloh* |
| 1967 | Emma Lathen *Murder Against the Grain* |
| 1968 | Peter Dickinson *Skin Deep* |
| 1969 | Peter Dickinson *A Pride of Heroes* |
| 1970 | Joan Fleming *Young Man, I Think You're Dying* |
| 1971 | James McClure *The Steam Pig* |
| 1972 | » Eric Ambler *The Levanter* |
| 1973 | Robert Littell *The Defection of A.J. Lewinter* |
| 1974 | Anthony Price *Other Paths to Glory* |
| 1975 | Nicholas Meyer *The Seven Per Cent Solution* |
| 1976 | » Ruth Rendell *A Demon in My View* |
| 1977 | John Le Carré *The Honourable Schoolboy* |
| 1978 | Lionel Davidson *The Chelsea Murders* |
| 1979 | » Dick Francis *Whip Hand* |
| 1980 | H.R.F. Keating *The Murder of the Maharajah* |
| 1981 | Martin Cruz Smith *Gorky Park* |
| 1982 | Peter Lovesey *The False Inspector Dew* |
| 1983 | John Hutton *Accidental Crimes* |
| 1984 | B.M. Gill *The Twelfth Juror* |
| 1985 | Paula Gosling *Monkey Puzzle* |
| 1986 | » Ruth Rendell *Live Flesh* |
| 1987 | » Barbara Vine *A Fatal Inversion* |
| 1988 | » Michael Dibdin *Ratking* |
| 1989 | » Colin Dexter *The Wench is Dead* |

1990 » Reginald Hill *Bones and Silence*

1991 » Barbara Vine *King Solomon's Carpet*

1992 » Colin Dexter *The Way Through the Woods*

1993 » Patricia Cornwell *Cruel and Unusual*

1994 » Minette Walters *The Scold's Bridle*

1995   Val McDermid *The Mermaids Singing*

1996   Ben Elton *Popcorn*

1997 » Ian Rankin *Black and Blue*

1998 » James Lee Burke *Sunset Limited*

1999   Robert Wilson *A Small Death in Lisbon*

2000   Jonathan Lethem *Motherless Brooklyn*

2001 » Henning Mankell *Sidetracked*

2002   José Carlos Somoza *The Athenian Murders*

2003 » Minette Walters *Fox Evil*

2004 » Sara Paretsky *Blacklist*

2005   Arnaldur Indridason *Silence of the Grave*

# INDEX

*10.30 From Marseilles* 107
*32 Cadillacs* 59
*42 Days for Murder* 15

*A is for Alibi* 60–61
*Absolution by Murder* 25, 123
*Act of Violence* 130
*Adam and Eve and Pinch Me* 130
Adams, Jane 150
*Advancement of Learning, An* 41
'Adventure of the Speckled Band,
The' 45
*Adventures of Race Williams,
The* 138
*Adventures of Sherlock Holmes,
The* 45, 46, 125
*Adventures of Solar Pons, The* 45
*After the Flood* 131
*Agatha Raisin and the Murderous
Marriage* 28
*Aground* 155
Aird, Catherine 17
*Alienist, The* 70
*All the Empty Places* 128

Allen, H. Warner 6
Allingham, Margery xiii, xiv, 1–2,
16, 133
*Almost Blue* 43
*Always Outnumbered, Always
Outgunned* 114
*Amazing Mrs Pollifax, The* 121
Ambler, Eric 2–3
*American Boy, The* 125
*American Tabloid* 48
Amis, Martin ix
*Amuse Bouche* 66
*Analyst, The* 70
*Angel Maker, The* 70
*Angel's Flight* 32, 99
*Angst-Ridden Executive, The* 113
*Anonymous Rex* 100
Apostolou, Anna 135
*Apothecary Rose, The* 123
*Appleby's End* 85
*Aristotle Detective* 135
Arjouni, Jakob 107
Arnott, Jake 128
*Art of Murder, The* 107

*As for the Woman* 84
*Ask for Me Tomorrow* 110
*Asphalt Jungle, The* 13
*Asta's Book* 148
*Athenian Murders, The* 135
Avallone, Max 138

*Back Spin* 29
*Bad Chili* 72
*Bad Company* 66
*Bad Guys* 98
Bailey, H.C. 133
Baldacci, David 70
Ball, John 115
Ballard, W.T 88
*Baltimore Blues* 61
*Bandits* 95
*Bannerman Solution, The* 145
Bardin, John Franklin xx, 4–5
Barnes, Linda 61
Barr, Nevada 78
Barre, Richard 92, 103
*Barred Window, The* 150
Baxt, George 66, 88
*Be Cool* 72
*Beast in View* 75, 109–110
*Beast Must Die, The* xix, 6–7
Beaton, M.C. 28
*Bedelia* 17, 18
*Bee-Keeper's Apprentice, The* 47

*Before the Fact* 84
Behm, Marc 100
*Behold This Woman* 57
*Beneath the Blonde* 66
*Beneath the Skin* 150
*Benson Murder Case, The* xiv
Bentley, E.C xiii, 5–6
Bergman, Andrew 89
Berkeley, Anthony 6, 83
Bidulka, Anthony 66
*Big Bamboo, The* 89
*Big Bow Mystery, The* 17, 97
*Big City Girl* 154
*Big Knockover, The* 15
*Big Nowhere, The* 48
*Big Sleep, The* 19
*Big Switch, The* 48
Billingham, Mark 70
*Birdman* 70
*Birthmarks* 61
*Bishop in the West Wing, The* 25
*Bitter Chill, A* 135
*Bitter Medicine* 61
*Black Alibi* 158
*Black Angel, The* 158
*Black Betty* 114
*Black and Blue* 125–126
*Black Cherry Blues* 12
*Black Curtain, The* 158
*Black Dahlia, The* 32, 47–48

*Black Dog* 76
*Black Echo, The* 31–32
*Black Ice Score, The* 139
*Black is the Fashion for Dying* 89
Black Mask magazine xviii, xv, 14, 19, 55
*Black Orchids* 141
*Black Path of Fear, The* 158
*Black Sunday* 68
*Blackboard Jungle, The* 97
*Blackwater* 106
*Blackwater Sound* 62, 63, 153
Blake, Nicholas xix, 6–7
*Blanche Cleans Up* 115
*Bleak House* 31
Blincoe, Nicholas 128
*Blind Eye, A* 63
Block, Lawrence xx, 8–9, 145, 158
*Blonde on the Street Corner, The* 158
*Blood Mud* 33, 73
Bludis, Jack 48
*Blue Bayou* 105
*Body Farm, The* 35
*Body Language* 62, 63, 66
*Body of Evidence* 35
*Bone Collector, The* 32
*Bonecrack* 54
*Bones of Coral* 63
Bonfiglioli, Kyril 72

*Bons and Silence* 75
Booth, Stephen 76
*Bordersnakes* 39, 40, 48
*Bottoms, The* 89–90
Boucher, Anthony 16, 89, 141
*Bourbon Street Blues* 66
Box, Edgar (Gore Vidal) 66
*Boy Who Never Grew Up, The* 89
Brackett, Leigh 18
Braddon, Mary Elizabeth 31
Brand, Christianna 27
Brett, Simon 28, 142
*Briarpatch* 145
*Bride Wore Black, The* 58, 157–158
Brookmyre, Christopher 72, 126
Brown, Fredric 9–10, 158
Browne, Howard 20
Buchanan, Edna 71, 153
*Bum's Rush, The* 52
*Bunny Lake is Missing* 18
*Burglar Who Thought He Was Bogart, The* 9
*Buried for Pleasure* 38, 85
Burke, James Lee 11–12, 40, 156
Burn Marks 116
Burnett, W.R. 13
*Burning Plain, The* 66
Burns, Ron 135
*Burnt Orange Heresy, The* 153
*Busman's Honeymoon* 132

Butler, Gwendoline  38, 87
*Butterfly, The*  13

*Cabal*  43
Cain, James M.  12–13, 147
Cain, Paul  14–15
*Caleb Williams*  x
*California Fire and Life*  95
*California Girl*  29
*California Roll*  103
*Call the Dying*  41
*Called by a Panther*  21
*Cambridge Murders, The*  38
Cameron, Jeremy  128
Camilleri, Andrea  43
Campbell, Robert  48
*Canary Murder Case, The*  141
Carlotto, Massimo  107
Carr, Caleb  47, 70
Carr, John Dickson  xix, 15–16, 47, 97
*Case of the Abominable Snowman, The*  8
*Case of the Baker Street Irregulars, The*  89
*Case of the Crumpled Knave, The*  141
*Case of the Dancing Sandwiches, The*  10
*Case of the Gilded Fly, The*  2, 38

*Case of the Glamorous Ghost, The*  55
*Case of the Hesitant Hostess, The*  55
*Case of the Howling Dog, The*  55
*Case of the Locked Key, The*  16
*Case of the Sulky Girl, The*  55
*Case of the Terrified Typist, The*  54–55
Caspary, Vera  17–18
*Cassidy's Girl*  57
*Cast a Yellow Shadow*  145
*Cast, In Order of Disappearance*  142
*Catch-22*  151
Caudwell, Sarah  57
Caunitz, William  98, 151
*Cavalier's Cup, The*  17
Cecil, Henry  68
*Certain Justice, A*  57
Chandler, Raymond  vi, xv, 12, 13, 14, 15, 19–20, 39, 51, 102, 103, 114, 117, 118
Chase, James Hadley  22–23
*Cheshire Moon, The*  51
Chesterton, G.K.  vi, xiii, xiv, 5, 15, 24–25, 46
Cheyney, Peter  23, 138
Child, Lee  81

*Chimney Sweeper's Boy, The* 148, 150

*Chinese Orange Mystery, The* 16

*Choirboys, The* 98, 150–151

Christie, Agatha vi, xiii, xiv, xv, xvi. 17, 26–28, 107, 121

*Church of Dead Girls, The* 90

*Cimarron Rose* 12

*City Called July, A* 21

*City of the Horizon* 121

*City Primeval* 51

Clancy, Tom xix

Clare, Alys 123

Clark, Alfred Gordon 67

*Clerical Errors* 25

*Clockers* 73

*Close Quarters* 56

*Clubbable Woman, A* 75

Coben, Harlan 28–29, 35, 51, 92

Cody, Liza 61

Coe, Tucker, 138, 139

Coel, Margaret 25

*Coffin Dancer, The* 70

*Coffin for Pandora, A* 38

*Cold Case* 61

*Cold Day for Murder, A* 78

*Cold is the Grave* 130, 131

*Cold Red Sunrise, A* 88

*Cold Touch of Ice, A* 121

*Cold War Swap, The* 144

Collins, Max Allen 21, 138

Collins, Wilkie xi, 30–31

*Colombian Mule, The* 107

*Colour of Murder, The* 141, 142

*Come Away, Death* 110–111

*Come Back Dead* 89

*Comeback* 54

*Common Murder* 61

*Concrete Blonde, The* 32, 37

Connelly, Michael 9, 31–32, 35, 36, 37, 48, 99, 131

Constantine, K.C. xix, 33–34, 73, 92

*Contents Under Pressure* 71

Cook, Christopher 156

Cook, Robin 127

*Cop Hater* xvii

*Cop Killer* 98

Cornwell, Patricia xviii, 34–35

*Cotton Comes to Harlem* 79

*Country of Old Men, A* 66

Cox, Anthony Berkeley xvii, 83

Craft, Michael 66

Crais, Robert 12, 29, 35–37

*Crazy Kill, The* 115

*Crime and Punishment* ix

*Crime at Black Dudley, The* xiii

*Crime School* 99

*Crimson, Twins, The* 113

Crispin, Edmund xvi, 2, 16, 37–38, 85

*Crocodile on the Sandbank* 120–121

Crofts, Freeman Wills 17

Crombie, Deborah 131

*Crooked Hinge, The* 16

*Crooked Man, The* 12

Crumley, James 39–40, 48

*Crust on Its Uppers, The* 127

Cullin, Mitch 47

Curzon, Clare 42

*Cut to Black* 42

*Cybeline Conspiracy, The* 135

D'Amato, Barbara 116

*Daffodil Affair, The* 38

*Dain Curse, The* 63, 64

Daly, Carroll John xv, 138

*Dance at the Slaughterhouse, A* 9

*Dancing Bear* 40

*Dancing in the Dark* 88

Daniel, Glyn 38

Dannay, Frederick xv

*Dark Coffin, A* 87

*Dark Passage* 57–58, 147

*Darkest Fear* 29

*Darkness More Than Night, A* 9, 32

*Darkness, Take My Hand* 92

*Daughter of Time, The* 143, 144

Davidson, Lionel 3

Davis, Lindsey 134

Davis, Norbert 10

Dawson, Janet 61

*Day of Wrath* 103

Day-Lewis, Cecil 7

*Dead Calm* 154–155

*Dead Cert* 53–54

*Dead Lagoon* 42–43

*Dead Man Upright* 128

*Dead Man's Dance* 51

*Dead Men's Morris* 111

*Dead of Jericho, The* 40–41

*Dead Ringer, The* 10

*Dead Secret, The* 31

*Dead Silent* 51

*Dead Sit Round in a Ring, The* 42

*Dead Skip* 59

*Deader the Better* 52

*Deadeye* 54

*Deadly Edge* 139

*Deadly Percheron, The* xx, 4–5

*Deadly Shade of Gold, A* 52, 102

*Deal Breaker* 28, 29

*Death at the Bar* 111

*Death Beyond the Nile* 121

*Death and the Chapman* 123

*Death Comes as the End* 121

*Death and the Dancing Footman* 108

*Death of a Doll* 18

*Death From a Top Hat* 17

*Death of a Ghost*  2, 133

*Death of a Hawker*  107

*Death of a Hollow Man*  108

*Death in Holy Orders*  86, 87, 133

*Death at La Fenice*  93

*Death and the Maiden*  42, 111, 130

*Death of Monsieur Gallet, The*  136

*Death on the Nile*  27

*Death at the President's Lodging*  85

*Death in a Strange Country*  92–93

*Death of Sweet Mister*  155, 156

*Death's Bright Angel*  87

*Death's Jest Book*  76

*Deaver, Jeffery*  32, 70

*Deeds of the Disturber, The*  121

*Deep Blue Goodbye, The*  101–102

*Deep Pockets*  61

*Déjà Dead*  35

*Delta Star, The*  151

*Demolition Angel*  37

*Depths of the Forest, The*  107

Derleth, August  45

*Detective is Dead, The*  126

*Devil in a Blue Dress*  21, 79, 113–114

*Devil and the Dolce Vita, The*  93

*Devil at Saxon Wall, The*  110

*Devil Take the Blue-Tail Fly*  5

*Devil's Home on Leave, The*  127–128

Dexter, Colin  40–41, 130, 144

*Dialogues of the Dead*  75–76

*Diamond Bikini, The*  10, 155

Dibdin, Michael  xix, 42–43, 47

Dickens, Charles  31, 82

Dickson, Carter (John Dickson Carr)  16, 17

*Dig My Grave Deep*  64

Dine, S.S. Van  xiv, 141

*Dirty Tricks*  43

*Disappearance of Sherlock Holmes, The*  47

Dobyns, Stephen  54, 90

*Dogs of Riga, The*  106

Doherty, Paul  121, 123

*Dominations*  133

*Don't Ask*  139

*Don't Lie to Me*  139

*Don't Look Back*  106

*Don't Point That Thing at Me*  72

Dorsey, Tim  63, 89, 153

Doss, James D.  78

Dostoevsky, Fyodor  ix

*Double Indemnity*  12–13

*Double Whammy*  71, 102, 153

*Down by the River Where the Dead Men Go*  22, 119

*Down There*  58

*Downriver*  49

Doyle, Sir Arthur Conan  vi, xii, 44–46, 47, 81, 82, 125

*Dr Jekyll and Mr Holmes*  47
*Dr Thorndyke's Casebook*  25
*Dreadful Lemon Sky, The*  63
*Dream Stalker, The*  25
Dreher, Sarah  66
*Drink Before the War, A*  92, 119
*Drop Shot*  37
Duffy, Stella  66
Dunant, Sarah  61
Dunbar, Tony  12
*Dupe*  61
*Dust to Dust*  99

*E is for Evidence*  61, 116
Eco, Umberto  123
Edwards, Grace F.  115
Edwards, Michael  135
Edwards, Ruth Dudley  38
*Edwin of the Iron Shoes*  116
*Egyptologist, The*  121
*Eight Million Ways to Die*  9
*Eighty Million Eyes*  98
Ekman, Kerstin  106
Elkins, Aaron  94
Ellroy, James  v, xvi, 32, 47–48
*End of Andrew Harrison, The*  17
Engel, Howard  21
*English Murder, An*  8, 68
*Enter a Murderer*  107
*Envious Casca*  27

*Epitaph for a Spy*  3
*Equal Danger*  113
Estleman, Loren D.  47, 49–50, 95
Evanovich, Janet  61, 72
*Everything You Have Give is Mine*  61
*Executioners, The*  102
*Exploits of Sherlock Holmes, The*  47
*Extenuating Circumstances*  9
*Eye of the Beholder, The*  100

*Fabulous Clipjoint, The*  9–10
*Face on the Cutting Room Floor, The*  xix, 99–100
*Faceless Killers*  106
*Fade Away*  51
*Fadeout*  65–66
Faherty, Terence  89
*Fallen Man, The*  78
*Falling Angel*  100
*False Pretences*  22
*Farewell, My Lovely*  20–21, 103, 114
*Fast One*  14–15
*Fatal Inversion, A*  147–148
*Fatal Remedies*  43
Faulkner, William  23
*Fear of the Dark*  115
*Fear to Travel*  56
*Fer-de-Lance*  141

Ferrigno, Robert  29, 51–52, 89

Fesperman, Dan  94

*Final Country, The*  40

*Final Curtain*  107

*Final Notice*  59

*'Final Problem, The'*  46

*Finding Moon*  94

*Fingering the Family Jewels*  66

*Finnegan's Week*  99

Finnis, Jane  135

*Firing Offence, A*  118–119

*First Lady*  105

Fisher, Steve  158

*Five Red Herrings*  111

*Flinch*  51–52

*Floater*  69

*Florida Roadkill*  63

*Florida Straits*  95, 153

*Flowers for the Judge*  16

*Fools in Town Are on Our Side, The*
    144–145

*Footsteps at the Lock*  6

*For Kicks*  54

*For the Sake of Elena*  38

Ford, G.M.  51–52, 63

Forester, C.S.  84

*Forfeit*  54

Forrest, Katherine V.  66

*Fortune Like the Moon*  123

Fossum, Karin  106

*Four Corners of Night*  80–81

*Four Just Men, The* xiii

*Franchise Affair, The*  143–144

Francis, Dick  xx, 53–54

Francome, John  54

Fraser, Antonia  38

*Freaky Deaky*  95

*Free Man of Colour, A*  115

Freeling, Nicolas  136

Freeman, R. Austin  xiii, 25

Fremlin, Celia  110

French, Nicci  150

*Frequent Hearses*  38

*Friday the Rabbi Slept Late*  25

Friedman, Kinky  72

*Friends of Eddie Coyle, The*  72–73

*From Doon With Death*  130

*From Potter's Field*  35

Fuentes, Eugenio  107

*Fugitive Pigeon, The*  72

*Full Whack*  128

*Fury*  52

Futrelle, Jacques  xiii, 46

*Fuzz*  98

Fyfield, Frances  148

Gaboriau, Emile  xi, xii, 82, 125

*Gallowglass*  148

*Gallows View*  130, 131

*Galton Case, The*  103

Garcia, Eric  100

Garcia-Aguilera, Carolina  153

Gardner, Erle Stanley  xviii, xx, 54–55, 98

*Gaudi Afternoon*  66

*Gaudy Night*  38, 133

Geagley, Brad  121

George, Elizabeth  38

*Germanicus Mosaic, The*  135

Gerritsen, Tess  35, 70

*Get Carter* (aka *Jack's Return Home*)  128

*Get Shorty*  89, 95

*Getaway, The*  153

*Ghosts of Morning*  103

*Ghostway, The*  78

Gilbert, Martin  xvi, 55–56, 68

Gill, Anton  121

Gillman, Dorothy  121

*Gitana*  113

*Glass Highway, The*  50

*Glass Key, The*  63–64

*Glitz*  95

'Gloria Scott, The'  45

*God Save the Child*  117–118

Goines, Donald  79

*Goldilocks*  153

*Gone Fishin'*  113, 114

*Gone Wild*  71

*Gone, Baby, Gone*  92

*Gone, No Forwarding*  58–59

*Goodbye Look, The*  103

Goodis, David  57–58, 147, 158

Gordon, Alan  123

Gores, Joe  58–59, 64

*Gorky Park*  94

Grafton, Sue  xix, 60–61, 116

Graham, Caroline  87, 108

*Grave Mistake, A*  27

Gray, Alex  42

*Greed and Stuff*  89

*Greek Coffin Mystery, The*  141

'Greek Interpreter, The'  46

Greeley, Andrew  25

*Green for Danger*  27

*Green Ice*  64

*Green Mummy, The*  82

*Green Ripper, The*  102

Greene, Graham  2, 3, 136

Greenleaf, Stephen  21

*Greenway, The*  150

*Greenwich Killing Time*  72

Greenwood, D.M.  25

Gregory, Susanna  123

Griffin, W.E.B.  99

*Grifters, The*  147

Grimes, Martha  108

Grisham, John  xix

*Gun for Sale, A*  136

*Gun, With Occasional Music*  100

Guttridge, Peter 72

*Hail, Hail, the Gang's All Here* 98
Hall, James W. 62–63, 71, 102, 153
Hall, Patricia 38
Hambly, Barbara 115
*Hamlet, Revenge!* 84–85, 108
Hammett, Dashiell xv, xvi, 15, 20, 21, 51, 58, 59, 63–64,
Handler, David 89
Haney, Lauren 121
*Hanging Valley, The* 41, 131
*Hangman's Beautiful Daughter, The* 90
*Hannibal* 69
Hansen, Joseph 65–66
*Happy Birthday, Turk* 107
*Hard Frost* 42
*Hard Women* 116
Harding, Paul 123
Hare, Cyril 8, 57, 67–68
Harris, Thomas 68–69
Harvey, John 42, 126
*Have Gat – Will Travel* 138
Hayder, Mo 70
Hayter, Sparkle 72
Haywood, Gar Anthony 115
*He Died With His Eyes Open* 128
*Headed for a Hearse* 72
Healy, Jeremiah 21

*Heartbreaker* 29, 51
Heath, W.L. 23, 155
*Heaven's Prisoners* 12
*Hell Hath No Fury* (aka *The Hot Spot*) 13, 155
*Hell of a Woman, A* 147
Heller, Joseph 151
*Hercule Poirot's Christmas* 17
Herren, Greg 66
Hewson, David 93
Heyer, Georgette 27
Hiaasen, Carl xviii, 70–71, 101, 102, 153
Higgins, George V. 33, 34, 72–73
*High Window, The* 20
Highsmith, Patricia xviii, xx, 74–75, 110, 147
Higson, Charles 128
*Hill Girl* 154
Hill, Reginald 41, 75–76, 131
Hillerman, Tony xix, 77–78, 94
Himes, Chester 78–79, 114, 115
*His Burial Too* 17
Hjortsberg, William 100, 125
Hoag, Tami 99
Hoeg, Peter 95
Holden, Craig 80–81
*Hollow Man, The* (*The Three Coffins*) xix, 15–16
*Hollywood and Levine* 89

*Hollywood Troubleshooter* 88
Holme, Timothy 93
Holton, Hugh 115
*Holy Disorders* 16
*Hombre* 94
*Hoodwink* 17
*Hostile Witness* 73
*Hot Rock, The* 139
*Hound of the Baskervilles,
   The* 44, 45
*Hour Game* 70
*Hours Before Dawn, The* 110
*House That Jack Built, The* 98
Household, Geoffrey 3
*How the Dead Live* 128
*How Like an Angel* 110
*Howard Hughes Affair, The* 88
Hughes, Dorothy B. 18
Hume, Fergus 31, 45, 81–82
*Hundredth Man, The* 70
Hunt, David 81
Hunter, Evan 97
*Hunter, The* (aka *Point Blank*)
   138–139
Hurley, Graham 42, 76

*I Am the Only Running Footman*
   108
*I, Claudia* 135
*I is for Innocent* 61

*I, The Jury* 137, 138
*I Wake Up Screaming* 158
*I Was Dora Suarez* 128
*Ice Harvest, The* 40
*If He Hollers Let Him Go* 78
*If I Should Die* 115
Iles, Francis xvii, 83–84
*Impostors* 73
*In a Dark House* 131
*In a Dry Season* 76, 130–131
*In the Electric Mist With
   Confederate Dead* 12
*In the Heat of the Night* 115
*In La-La Land We Trust* 48
*In a Lonely Place* 18
*In the Memory of the Forest* 94
*Indemnity Only* 61, 115–116
Indridason, Arnaldur 106
Innes, Michael xvi, 8, 38, 84–85, 108
*Innocence of Father Brown, The*
   24–25, 46
*Innocents, The* 92
*Inside Track* 54
*Investigators, The* 99
*It Walks by Night* 97
*Italian Secretary, The* 47
Izzi, Eugene 73, 98

James, Bill 42, 126
James, P.D xvi, 38, 75, 86–87, 57, 133

Jance, J.A. 99
Japrisot, Sebastien 107, 136
*Jar City* 106
Jardine, Quintin 42, 126
*Jazz Bird* 81
Jecks, Michael 123
*Jolie Blon's Bounce* 156
*Judas Goat, The* 118
*Judas Sheep, The* 131
*Judgement on Deltchev* 3

Kaminsky, Stuart M. 87–88, 99, 153
*Katwalk* 61
Katzenbach, John 70
Kellerman, Faye 70, 99
Kellerman, Jonathan 35
Kemelman, Harry 25
*Kentish Manor Mysteries, The* 141
Kerley, Jack 70
Kernick, Simon 128
Kerr, Philip 69
*Keys to the Street, The* 130
Kienzle, William X. 25
Kijewski, Karen 61
*Killer Inside Me, The* 146–147
*Killer's Choice* 98
*Killing Club, The* 105
*Killing Floor* 81
*Killings at Badger's Drift, The* 87
*Kinds of Love, Kinds of Death* 139

*King of the Rainy Country* 136
*King Suckerman* 119
King, Laurie 47
*Kiss the Girls* 69
*Kiss Me, Deadly* 137–138
*Kiss Tomorrow Goodbye* 58
*Kissing the Gunner's Daughter* 130
Klein, Zachary 40
Knight, Bernard 123
*Knots and Crosses* 126
Knox, Ronald xiv, 6
Koenig, Joseph 69

*La Brava* 94–95
*LA Confidential* 48,
*LA Quartet, The* 48
*LA Requiem* 37
*Lady Audley's Secret* 31
*Lady in the Car With Glasses and a Gun* 136
*Lady in the Lake, The* 21
*Laidlaw* 126
*Landscape With Dead Dons* 85
Lansdale, Joe R. 72, 89–90
Lanyon, Josh 66
Larkin, Philip 110
Lashner, William 73
*Last Bus to Woodstock* 40, 41

*Last Coyote, The* 48
*Last Detective, The* 41
*Last Good Kiss, The* 39–40
*Last Reminder* 42
*Last Sanctuary., The* 80
*Last Seen in Massilia* 134
*Last Seen Wearing* xvii, 99, 130
*Last Sherlock Holmes Story, The*
  43, 47
*Last Templar, The* 123
*Late-Night News, The* 107
Latimer, Jonathan 10, 72, 89
*Laughing Policeman, The* 106
*Laura* 17–18
*Laurels Are Poison* 38
Lawrence, David 42
Lawrence, Hilda 18
*League of Frightened Men, The*
  140–141
Lee, Manfred B. xv
Lehane, Dennis 12, 91–92, 119
Leon, Donna xix, 43, 92–93
Leonard, Elmore xvi, 51, 72, 73, 89,
  94–95, 153
*Leper of St Giles, The* 25
*Lerouge Affair, The* xi
Leroux, Gaston 96–97
*Let It Bleed* 126
Lethem, Jonathan 100
Lewin, Michael Z. 21

Lewis, Ted 128
*Lie in the Dark* 94
*Lieberman's Law* 99
Lilly, Greg 66
*Lion in the Valley* 121
Lippman, Laura 61
*Listen to the Silence* 78
*Little Dog Laughed, The* 66
*Little Sister, The* 21, 118
*Little Yellow Dog, A* 22, 114
Llewellyn, Sam 54
Lochte, Dick 37, 105
*Locked Room, The* 17
*Lolita Man, The* 42
*London Boulevard* 128
*London Fields* ix
*Long Cold Fall, A* 119
*Long Firm, The* 128
*Long Goodbye, The* 20
*Long-Legged Fly, The* 79
*Looking for Rachel Wallace* 118
*Lost Get-Back Boogie, The* 11
*Love Lies Bleeding* 38
Lovesey, Peter 41
Lucarelli, Carlo 43
*Lullaby Town* 37
*Lust is No Lady* 138
Lutz, John 153
Lyons, Arthur 21, 22, 51, 118

MacDonald, John D. xx, 52, 63, 101–102

MacDonald, Philip 8

Macdonald, Ross xvi, 20, 21, 39, 102–103, 109

Mackintosh, Josephine 143

*Madame Midas* 31, 82

*Magician's Tale, The* 81

*Maigret and the Burglar's Wife* 136

*Maigret and the Reluctant Witnesses* 136

*Maigret Sets A Trap* 135–136

*Maigret Travels South* 136

*Malice Aforethought* xvii, 83–84

*Mallory's Oracle* 35

Malone, Michael 104–105

*Maltese Falcon, The* 20, 21, 59, 63, 64

*Mama Black Widow* 79

*Man of Maybe Half-a-Dozen Faces, The* 100

*Man Who Killed Himself, The* 142

*Man Who Knew Too Much, The* 25

*Man Who Liked to Look at Himself, The* 33–34, 92

*Man Who Liked Slow Tomatoes, The* 34

*Man Who Watched the Trains Go By, The* 136

*Man With the Getaway Face, The* 139

*Mandala of Sherlock Holmes, The* 47

Mankell, Henning 105–106

Mann, Jessica 121

Markaris, Petros 107

Maron, Margaret 105

Marsh, Ngaio xiv, xv, xvi, 2, 27, 107–108, 111, 133, 142

*Marshal and the Murderer, The* 93

Marston, A.E. 123

Martell, Dominic 113

*Martians, Go Home* 10

*Martin Hewitt, Investigator* 46

*Mask of Dimitrios, The* 2–3

*Mask of Ra, The* 121

*Mask of Red Death, The* 125

Massey, Sujata 94

*Matricide at St Martha's* 38

Maxim, John R. 145

McBain, Ed xvii, 97–98, 153

McCabe, Cameron xix, 99–100

McClure, James 94

McCoy, Horace 13, 58

McCrumb, Sharyn 90

McDermid, Val 61, 66, 70, 76, 131

McIlvanney, William 126

McLeod, Charlotte 121

*McNally's Luck* 118

*McNally's Secret* 153
*Mean High Tide* 63
*Medusa* 43
*Meeting of Minds, A* 42
*Memoirs of Sherlock Holmes, The* 45–46
Mencken, H.L. xv
*Mermaids Singing, The* 70
*Miami Blues* 152–153
*Miami, It's Murder* 153
*Mildred Pierce* 13
*Mildred Pierced* 88
Millar, Kenneth xvi, xviii, 102
Millar, Margaret 75, 109–110
Millett, Larry 47
*Mind of Mr J.G. Reeder, The* 25
*Mirror Crack'd From Side to Side, The* 28
*Miss Silver Intervenes* 28
*Miss Smilla's Feeling for Snow* 94
*Missing* 22
*Missionary Stew* 145
Mitchell, Gladys xvi, 38, 110–111
*Mona* 158
*Monk's Hood* 123
*Monkey's Raincoat, The* 35–36
*Monsieur LeCoq* 125
Montalbán, Manuel Vázquez 111–112
Montgomery, Bruce 37
*Moon in the Gutter, The* 58

*Moonstone, The* xi, 30–31
*Morbid Taste for Bones, A* 123
*More Work for the Undertaker* 2
Morrison, Arthur xiii, 46
Mortimer, John 57
*Mortality Play* 123
Mosley, Walter xix, 21, 22, 79, 113–114
*Moth* 114
*Motor City Blue* 50, 95
*Mouse in the Mountain, The* 10
*Moving Finger, The* 28
*Moving Target, The* xvi, 20, 102–103
*Moving Toyshop, The* 37–38
*Mrs Murphy's Underpants* 10
*Mucho Mojo* 90
Muller, Marcia 60, 61, 78, 116
*Mummy Case, The* 121
*Murder Among Children* 139
*Murder is Announced, A* 27–28
*Murder on the Appian Way, A* 134
*Murder in the Central Committee* 111–112
*Murder Exchange, The* 128
*Murder Gone Mad* 8
*Murder in Macedon, A* 135
*Murder in the Madhouse* 10
*Murder in Mesopotamia* 27
*Murder Must Advertise* 2, 132, 133
*Murder on the Orient Express* 27

*Murder at the Panionic Games* 135

*Murder in the Place of Anubis* 121

*Murder of Roger Ackroyd, The*
26–27

*Murder by Tradition* 66

*Murder on the Yellow Brick Road*
87–88

*Murder at the Vicarage, The* 28

'*Murders in the Rue Morgue, The*'
x, 17, 124

'*Musgrave Ritual, The*' 45

*My Dark Places* 48

*My Friend Maigret* 136

*My Gun is Quick* 23, 138

*Mysterious Affair at Styles, The* xiii

*Mystery of a Hansom Cab, The* 45,
81–82

*Mystery of Edwin Drood, The* 82

'*Mystery of Marie Roget, The*' x,
125

*Mystery of Orcival, The* xi, 82

*Mystery of the Yellow Room, The*
96–97

*Mystic River* 12, 91–92


Nabb, Magdalen 93

*Nag's Hook* 16

*Name of the Rose, The* 123

*Name Withheld* 99

*Narcissist's Daughter, The* 80

Nathan, George Jean xv

*Native Tongue* 71

*Nature of the Beast* 148

Nava, Michael 66

Neel, Janet 87

Neely, Barbara 115

*Neon Rain, The* 11–12

*Never Cross a Vampire* 88

*Never Somewhere Else* 42

*Nevermore* 125

*New Centurions, The* 150, 151

*New Hope for the Dead* 153

*Nice Class of Corpse, A* 28

*Nice Derangement of Epitaphs,
A* 123

*Nick's Trip* 40

*Night of the Jabberwock* 10

*Night Passage* 118

*Night at the Vulcan* 107, 142

*Night of Wenceslas, The* 3

*Nightcrawlers* 128

*Nightfall* 57, 58

*Nightingale Gallery, The* 123

*Nine Tailors, The* 87, 131–132

*Nineteen Seventy Four* 128

*No Bail for the Judge* 68

*No Good From a Corpse* 18

*No. 1 Ladies' Detective Agency,
The* 94

*No Laughing Matter* 72

*No Orchids for Miss Blandish*  22
*No Pockets in a Shroud*  13
*Noble Radiance, A*  93
*Nobody's Perfect*  139
Noll, Ingrid  107
Norbu, Jamyang  47
*Nothing Man, The*  58
Noyer, Albert  135

*O'Connell, Carol*  35
*O is for Outlaw*  61, 99
*Off With His Head*  107–108, 133
*Old Man in the Corner, The*  25
*Oliver Twist*  ix
*Olympic Death, An*  113
*On Beulah Height*  76, 131
*One Corpse Too Many*  122–123
*One to Count Cadence*  39
*One False Move*  29, 92
*One Fearful Yellow Eye*  102
*One Fine Day in the Middle of the
    Night*  71
*One for the Money*  61
*One Police Plaza*  98, 151
*Ones You Do, The*  156
*Onion Field, The*  150
*Opening Night*  107
*Orange Crush*  153
Orczy, Baroness  25
*Original Sin*  86, 87

Orwell, George  23
*Other People's Money*  21, 118
*Out of Sight*  95
*Outfit, The*  139
*Outlaws*  73
*Over the Edge*  35
*Oxford Blood*  38

*Paint it Black*  128
Paretsky, Sara  60, 61, 115–116
Pargeter, Edith  122
Parker, Robert B.  vii, 21, 51, 117–118
Parker, T. Jefferson  29
*Past Tense*  21
Patterson, James  69
Pattison, Eliot  94
Pavón, Francisco García  113
Pawson, Stuart  42, 131
*Payment Deferred*  84
Peace, David  128
Pearce, Michael  121
Pearson, Ridley  70
Pelecanos, George  22, 40, 115,
    118–119
*People of Darkness*  78
*Perdition, USA*  114
Pérez-Reverte, Arturo  25
Peters, Elizabeth  vi, 120–121
Peters, Ellis  25, 122–123
Petievich, Gerald  151

*Phantom of the Opera, The* 97

*Pharmacist, The* 107

Phillips, Arthur 121

Phillips, Gary 79, 114

Phillips, Scott 40

*Philosophical Investigation, A* 69

Piper, Evelyn 18

*Place of Execution, A* 76

*Plague on Both Your Houses, A* 123

Poe, Edgar Allan vi, x, xii, 17, 124–25

Poet, The 32

*Poisoned Chocolates Case, The* 84

*Poodle Springs* 21, 118

*Pop.1280* 147

*Postman Always Rings Twice, The* 12, 13, 147

*Postmortem* 34–35

Powers, Charles 94

Prather, Richard S. 138

*Prayers for the Assassin* 51

*Prayers for the Dead* 99

*Prayers for Rain* 92

Price, Richard 73

Pronzini, Bill 17, 22, 128

'*Purloined Letter, The*' x, 125

Queen, Ellery xv, 16, 141

*Queer Kind of Death, A* 66

*Quite Ugly One Morning* 126

Rabe, Peter 64

Radley, Sheila 42, 130

*Rage in Harlem, A* 78–79, 114

Rankin, Ian vii, xix, 125–126

*Rare Coin Score, The* 139

*Rat on Fire, The* 34

Rawson, Clayton 17

Raymond, Derek 127–128

Raymond, Réné Brabazon 22

*Real Cool Killers, The* 79

*Rear Window* 157

Reaves, Sam 119

*Red Dragon* 68–69

*Red Harvest* 15, 63, 64

'*Red-Headed League, The*' 45

*Red Thumb Mark, The* xiii

Reichs, Kathy 35

Rendell, Ruth xvi, xx, 84, 147, 129–130

*Rendezvous in Black* 157, 158

*Report for Murder* 66

*Requiem, Requiem* 35

*Rest You Merry* 121

*Resurrection Men* 126

*Retreat From Oblivion* 57

*Return of Sherlock Holmes, The* 46

Rickman, Phil 25

*Riding the Rap* 73

*Right Hand of Amon, The* 121

*Right as Rain* 115

*Ripley's Game* 75
*Rising of the Moon, The* 110, 111
*River Girl* 154
*River Sorrow, The* 80, 81
Robb, Candace 123
*Robbers* 156
Roberts, John Maddox 135
Robinson, Lynda S. 121
Robinson, Peter 41, 76, 130–131
Robinson, Robert 85
*Rocksburg Railroad Murders, The* 33, 34
*Rogue Male* 3
*Roman Blood* 133–134
*Roman Nights* 135
*Rosary Murders, The* 25
Rowe, Rosemary 135
*Rum Punch* 95
*Rumpole of the Bailey* 57
Ruric, Peter 14
Russell, Jay 89

*Sacred* 92
*Sadie When She Died* 97–98
*Sailcloth Shroud, The* 155
Sallis, James 79, 114
*Samurai's Daughter, The* 94
*Sanctuary* 23
*Sanctuary Seeker, The* 123
Sanders, Lawrence 118, 153

Sandford, John 70
*Saratoga Headhunter* 54
*Satan in St Mary's* 123
*Savage Night* 155
Sayers, Dorothy L. v, xiii, xiv, xvi, 2, 38, 86, 87, 107, 111, 131–133
Saylor, Steven xix, 133–134
*Scattershot* 22
*Scavenger Hunt* 51, 89
Schechter, Harold 125
Sciascia, Leonardo 113
*Scold's Bridle, The* 150
Scoppettone, Sandra 61
*Scorpion Reef* 155
*Screaming Mimi, The* 10, 158
*Sculptress, The* 148–149
*Season for the Dead, A* 93
Sedley, Kate 123
*Seeking Whom He May Devour* 107
*Serenade* 13
*Seven Per Cent Solution, The* 45
*Seven Slayers* 14
*Seville Communion, The* 25
*Shadow on the Wall* 133
*Shaman Sings, The* 78
Shames, Laurence 71, 95, 153
*Shape of Dread, The* 61
*Shape of Snakes, The* 149, 150
*Shape of Water, The* 43
Shaw, Joseph (editor) xv

*She Came Too Late* 66

*Shroud for Grandmama, A* 5

*Shutter Island* 91, 92

*Sick Puppy* 71

*Sideswipe* 153

*Sidetracked* 105–106

*Sign of Four, The* xii, 44–45, 82

*Silence of the Lambs, The* 69

*Silk Stocking Murders, The* 6

*'Silver Blaze'* 45

*Silver Pigs, The* 134

Simenon, Georges 135–136

Simon, Roger L. 103

*Singing Sands, The* 144

*Singing in the Shrouds* 108

Sjöwall, Maj 17, 106

*Skeleton at the Feast* 38

*Skinflick* 66

*Skinner's Rules* 126

*Skinwalkers* 78

*Skull Beneath the Skin* 75

*Skull Mantra, The* 94

*Slayground* 139

*Sleeping Dog* 37

*Sleepyhead* 70

*Slight Trick of the Mind, A* 47

*Slim, Iceberg* 79

*Slow Burn* 52

*Small Death in Lisbon, A* 113

*Smallbone Deceased* 55–56, 68

*Smile on the Face of the Tiger, A* 50

*Smile of a Ghost* 25

*Smiler With the Knife, The* 8

Smith, Alexander McCall 94

Smith, Martin Cruz 94

*Some Buried Caesar* 141

*Something About a Soldier* 152

Somoza, José Carlos 107, 135

*Soul Circus* 119

*Southern Discomfort* 105

*Speaker of Mandarin, The* 130

*Spider Webs* 109

Spillane, Mickey 23, 137–138

*SPQR: The King's Gambit* 135

*Squall* 102

*Squall Line* 63

Staalesen, Gunnar 107

Stabenow, Dana 78

*Stain on the Snow, The* 136

*Stained White Radiance, A* 12, 40

*Staked Goat, The* 21

*Stalking the Angel* 37

*Stamboul Train* 3

Stark, Richard 138–139

*State of Denmark, A* 127

*Steam Pig, The* 94

Stewart, J.I.M. 84

*Stick* 94, 153

*Still Among the Living* 40

*Still Water*  42, 126

Stout, Rex  140–141

*Straight into Darkness*  70

Strand, The, magazine  xii, xiii, 45

*Strange Marriage*  65

*Stranger in My Grave, A*  110

*Strangers on a Train*  74, 110

*Street Players*  79

*Strip Jack*  126

*Strong Poison*  132, 133

*Study in Scarlet, A*  xii, 45, 81

*Sunburn*  71

*Sunset Express*  37

*Surfeit of Lampreys*  2, 107, 108

*Surgeon, The*  35, 70

*Swag*  94

*Sweet Forever, The*  119

Symons, Julian  x, xvi, 85, 99, 141–142


*Talented Mr Ripley, The*  74–75

*Tales of Mystery and Imagination*
    124

*Tampa Burn*  153

*Taste of Ashes, The*  20

*Taste for Death, A*  86–87

Taylor, Andrew  41, 125, 150

*Tell No One*  28–29

*Ten Thousand Islands*  102

*Tenant for Death*  67

Tey, Josephine  143–144

*The Hell You Say*  66

*Thief of Time, A*  77–78

*Thief Who Couldn't Sleep, The*  9,
    145

*Thin Man, The*  63, 64

*Thinking Machine, The*  46

*Thirteenth Night*  123

*This Man is Dangerous*  23

*This Way for a Shroud*  23

Thomas, Ross  144–145

Thompson, Jim  58, 146–147, 153, 155

*Three by Box*  66

*Three Pipe Problem, A*  141–142

*Three With a Bullet*  51

*Thrones*  133

*Thus Was Adonis Murdered*  57

*Tiger in the Smoke, The*  1–2

*Tiger by the Tail*  23

*Time's Witness*  105

Timlin, Mark  128

*To Live and Die in LA*  151

Todd, Marilyn  135

*Tomato Red*  155, 156

Torrey, Roger  15

*Touch of Death, A*  155

*Tourist Season*  70–71

*Toxic Shock*  116

*Track of the Cat*  78

*Tragedy at Law*  57, 67, 68

*Traitor's Purse*  2

Treat, Lawrence  xvii

Tremayne, Peter  25, 123

*Trent Intervenes*  6

*Trent's Last Case*  xiii, 5–6

*Tribal Secrets*  73

*Tropical Heat*  153

*Trouble is My Business*  15

*True Detective*  21

*Trunk Music*  32

*Tunnel Vision*  116

Turnbull, Peter  131

*Turnstone*  76

Turow, Scott  xviii

*Twenty Blue Devils*  94

*Twenty-Third Man, The*  111

*Twist at the End, A*  134

*Two for the Dough*  72

*Two for the Money*  138

*Two-Bear Mambo, The*  90


*Uncivil Season*  104–105

*Under the Bright Lights*  155–156

*Under Cover of Daylight*  62–63

*Underground Man, The*  22, 103

*Unkindness of Ravens, An*
   129–130

*Unsuitable Job for a Woman,
   An*  38, 87

Unsworth. Barry  123

*V for Victim*  xvii

Valin, Jonathan  22, 103

*Valley of Fear, The*  45

Vargas, Fred  107

*Vendetta*  93

*Vengeance*  153

*Vengeance is Mine*  137, 138

Vine, Barbara  xviii, 129, 147–148,
   150

*Vinnie Got Blown Away*  128

*Violent Crimes*  115

*Violent Saturday*  23, 155

*Violent Spring*  79

*Virgin in the Ice, The*  123

*Voodoo, Ltd*  145

*Voodoo River*  12

Vukcevich, Ray  100


Wahlöö, Per  17, 106

*Wake-Up, The*  51

*Walk Among the Tombstones, A*  9

Wallace, Edgar  xiii, 25

Walsh, Jill Paton  38, 133

Walsh, Marcie  105

Walters, Minette  xviii, xix, 84,
   148–149

Wambaugh, Joseph  98, 99, 150–151

Waugh, Hillary  xvii, 99

*Wax Apple*  139

*Way Through the Woods, The* 41
*Way We Die Now, The* 153
*We All Killed Grandma* 10
*Weight of the Evidence, The* 8
*Wench is Dead, The* 144
Wentworth, Patricia 28
Westlake, Donald E. xviii, 72, 138, 139
Wetering, Jan Willem van de 107
*What's a Girl Gotta Do?* 72
*When the Sacred Ginmill Closes* 8–9
*When the Wind Blows* 67–68
*Where the Bodies Are Buried* 61
*Whiskey River* 50
*White Jazz* 48
*White Murder* 134
*White Priory Murders, The* 16
White, Randy Wayne 102
Whitfield, Raoul 64
*Who In Hell Is Wanda Fuca?* 51–52
*Widening Gyre, The* 51
*Wild Town* 147
Willeford, Charles 152–153
*William Powell and Myrna Loy Murder Case, The* 88

Williams, Charles 10, 13, 154–155
Wilson, Barbara 66
Wilson, Edmund 12
Wilson, Robert 113
Wingfield, R.D. 42
Wings, Mary 66
Winslow, Don 95
*Winter's Bone* 155
*Wisdom of Father Brown, The* 25
Wishart, David 134
*Wolves of Savernake, The* 123
*Woman in White, The* xi, 30, 31
*Wonderful Years, Wonderful Years* 73
Woodrell, Daniel xix, 155–156
Woolrich, Cornell 58, 157–158
*Writing on the Wall, The* 107
*Wrong Case, The* 39, 40
Wyndham Case, The 38

*Year of the Hyenas* 121
Yorke, Margaret 130
*Your Deal, My Lovely* 138

Zangwill, Israel 17, 97